SHADOWS OF RAZORHURST

CRAIG STANTON

SHADOWS OF RAZORHURST

First published by Oceaniacom Press 2025
A division under Oceaniacom Pty Ltd.
www.oceaniacom.com

Shadows of Razorhurst

Copyright © 2025 by CRAIG STANTON

ISBN (Print): 978-1-923113-12-1
ISBN (Ebook): 978-1-923113-13-8

Cover design by Craig Stanton

**To my Family
For bringing me back to life.
To Michelle,
For making it worthwhile.**

**This book was written on Dharug land.
Always was, always will be.**

SHADOWS OF RAZORHURST

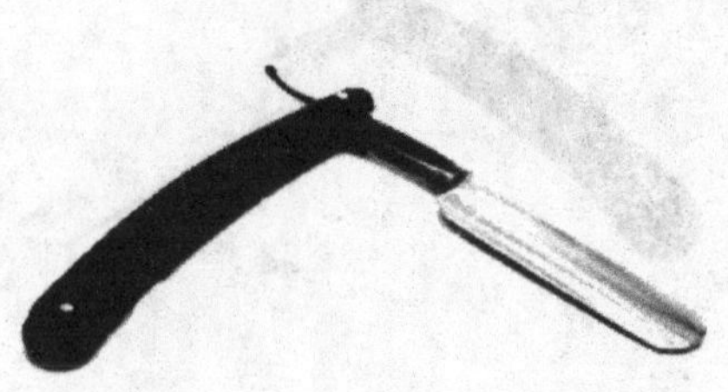

BY

CRAIG STANTON

CONTENTS

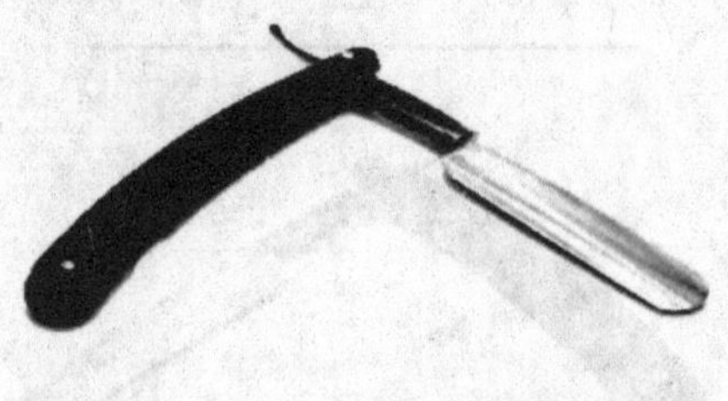

From the Casebook of Patrick Dolan

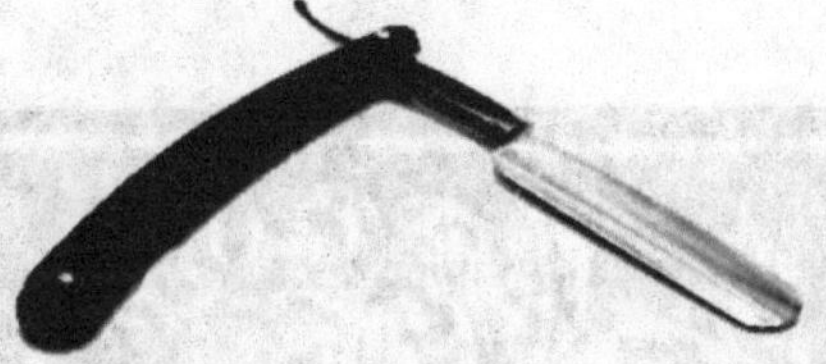

"Listen to them—the children of the night. What music they make!"
-*Dracula*, Chapter 2, 1897

I.

"THE DEVIL DRIVES"

THE DEVIL DRIVES

"NEEDS MUST, WHERE THE DEVIL DRIVES..."

-TRADITIONAL SAYING

I'd had my lights punched out before. Plenty of times. But never by a seventeen-year-old girl.

I came to in a pile of sawdust redolent of stale beer and human by-products. My hat covered my face, for which I was grateful, and I was lying on my back. My shoes were being slowly toasted by a band of sunlight rolling across the floor. I probed my molars one by one with my tongue—definitely rattled, but all still present and accounted-for.

I heard the clanking of a bucket and the slopping of water: I sat up slowly, letting my hat fall into my lap.

'Well, I see you survived,' a voice rasped.

I squinted in the morning sunshine. The roller blinds were at half-mast, glowing redly, and dust motes swam in the honey-coloured beams which flowed beneath them. Across the room from me was a hunched-over old man in threadbare clothes, munching a cigarette and leaning heavily on a broom. His bright gaze made me think his eyes were made of glass, but that couldn't be right. Not both of them. He craned his neck and spat noisily into a bucket of suds next to his feet.

'You gonna git movin'?' he asked, ''cause I gotta mop this joint down fer ternight. I only let you stay 'cause he asked me to.' He nodded towards the bar where liquid sunshine slammed slowly into the boot-scuffed woodwork beyond the brass rail. Limned in gold was a pair of worn, pointed shoes, bedecked in pearl-grey spats, on feet attached to legs crossed at the ankles. They un-crossed as I squinted harder and their owner stood up from leaning against the marble top. Using a nearby barstool, I followed suit. Cramming my hat on my head, I raised a shielding hand to take in this stranger.

He was a little under average height, hatchet-faced and swarthy. His black hair was unfashionably long—presuming of course that he wasn't a professional musician of some type—and he affected a pencil-thin moustache. He wore a grey suit, a shade or two darker than his spats, over which was thrown a dark coat. His gloved hands held a homburg hat and a black cane.

'I know you?' I said, rubbing my stubbly and tender jaw.

'Not yet,' he answered brightly, his English coloured with a faint European twang. 'At the moment I'm just the fellow who paid for your night's accommodation—such as it was.'

The old bloke with the bucket chuckled and began pushing sawdust with his broom.

'Well, thanks, I guess,' I said shrugging my shoulders. 'What makes you so interested in my welfare?'

Before answering, he planted his cane on the floor and smiled out towards the waiting day. A number of small metallic objects, attached to fine gold and silver chains around his wrists, rattled against the carved head of his walking stick.

'You and I,' he said, turning his gaze upon me, 'are looking for the same person.'

* * *

I was still spluttering angrily some minutes later as we stepped out onto the street.

'This was supposed to be an exclusive contract!' I fumed. 'If someone else was going to be brought in on the case, that was to be at my discretion. I can't do my job if I'm tripping over someone else's feet all the time!'

The nattily dressed man turned suddenly to face me, raising conciliatory hands.

'Now, now,' he soothed, 'let me be clear about this. We're looking for the same person, but we're not working the same case. And we certainly aren't in the employ of the same person.'

'So, you're not getting bankrolled by Danvers?'

He shook his head. 'I'm working for quite a different individual,' he said. 'One might say a higher power.'

'Might one?' I threw a cigarette in my mouth and lit it with the lighter from my coat pocket.

'The Danvers girl is the point where our two investigations intersect,' he continued. 'You are trying to return her to her parents; she has information that I need to obtain.'

I exhaled slowly, smoke streaming in two jets from my nostrils, while my gaze narrowed. 'Are you suggesting that we collaborate?'

His eyes twinkled. 'I definitely think that it would be worth our while.'

I ashed my smoke on the pavement and leaned back on my heels. 'Really?' I rumbled.

'Absolutely,' was his response. 'You have certain physical advantages over me that I feel could be useful, while I possess a wealth of knowledge about the current situation which should prove invaluable...'

'...For which you would command how much of the fee, d'you reckon?' I put some venom in the words as I lobbed them out.

For an instant, his face blanked as he registered what I was saying. Then he chuckled and waved a gloved hand.

'Mr Dolan,' he said, 'whatever arrangement you have made with Mr Danvers, that is your business entirely. I have, as I said, my own—backers—and my own contract. I seek no remuneration from your involvement; it simply seems to me that our combined forces would further both our objectives that much more greatly than if—as you say—we trod on each other's toes...'

'I usually work alone,' I interjected.

'...And you have no idea what you're getting into,' he finished.

I glared at him. 'I've an idea that I'm tracking down the wayward daughter of a wealthy businessman, a girl who's keen to leave her boring North Shore lifestyle of tennis and tea parties for a bit of excitement on the wrong side of the Harbour. I've done this a dozen times, easy—you find 'em, follow 'em, and then sweep in to grab 'em just when they've bitten off more than they can chew; then you drag 'em home, grateful, to a tearful mama. Tell me again that I don't know my own job!'

He pulled a keychain from his vest pocket and used it to point towards a black Oldsmobile parked by the kerb next to us.

'How often does the girl knock you unconscious just as you're adopting the white knight routine? Shall we?' He checked the road for traffic then strode quickly around to the driver's side door and slipped in. Seconds later, the passenger side door flew open, and his voice piped out over the road noise:

'Come along, Mr Dolan! Our quarry has about eight hours' head start on us. We've got some catching-up to do!'

I bent down and glared in at him. Then I flicked my cigarette away and squeezed into the car. It doesn't matter what make of vehicle it is, I never have enough room to be comfortable. I struggled around for a bit then slammed the door shut.

'Say!' I said, 'how exactly do you know my name?'

In reply, he raised an index finger then fumbled in an inside coat pocket with the other hand. When it emerged once more, it held my wallet.

'Please excuse the liberty,' he said, 'but given the choice of myself or the bartender acting as guardian, I felt that you'd prefer I looked after this for you.'

The moment I'd seen it, I did that stupid routine of patting all of my pockets in order to ascertain that what I was seeing was real. Realising the futility of this manoeuvre however, I stopped then retrieved my wallet with a grunt. He was right—falling unconscious in a King's Cross pub is the quickest way to discover yourself waking up naked in a Darlinghurst back lane… if you wake up at all. Nevertheless, I checked the contents, then tucked it away.

'And what do I call you?' I growled.

'Anton,' he replied, pulling the car out into the street, 'Anton Vadász.'

* * *

We drifted off into the traffic and I took stock of my surroundings. The interior of the car looked as though someone spent a great deal of time within it: there were leather-bound books on the dashboard and a kind of magazine rack stuffed with ledgers and newspapers divided the floorspace between me and Vadász; an enamel mug with two pencils and a fountain-pen inside it, rattled in a wire holder hanging between the glove box and the instrument panel; a thermos flask rolled around on the floor, bumping against my shoes.

'Excuse the mess,' said Vadász, 'when I'm on assignment my car becomes a sort of second office.'

'Certainly seems cosy,' I answered. 'What's that?' I pointed at a blue glass disc hanging with a pendant tassel from the rear-vision mirror.

He turned it over in his fingers, revealing that the forward-facing surface bore a white circle with a black dot in the middle of it.

'This is a charm to deflect the Evil Eye,' he informed me.

I shot him an appraising look.

'Many folks trying to put the whammy on you?' I asked.

'Not often,' he smirked, 'but I like to keep all my bases covered.'

I continued my examination. What I assumed was a petrol gauge, turned out to be a small votive image of the Virgin Mary in a circular gold frame; Palm Sunday crosses stuck out at neat angles from the sun visors; a St. Christopher medal swung from the gear shift. Through the windshield I could see that the standard hood mascot had been replaced by a brass statue of some elephant-headed deity.

'I get the impression you're kinda superstitious,' I observed, pulling my cigarettes from my coat pocket.

'Not at all,' he replied. 'I just like to have all the options open to me. That won't work, by the way.' He pointed at my lighter.

I cocked an eyebrow at him and went ahead and tried it anyway. True to what I'd just been told, the lighter refused to spout flame. Instead, the interior of the car faintly glowed, a fine network tracery of lines and sigils, pulsing orange from a point directly above me on the ceiling, swept across the vehicle's interior surface and faded once more from view. Annoyed, I tried lighting up a few more times rapidly before Vadász's hand clamped down over mine.

'The car resists fire,' he said, 'you're just wasting your time.'

'"Resists fire"?' I growled, 'how does that work? Some kinda asbestos?'

'Not really,' he responded vaguely, 'suffice it to say that fires inside the car are put into abeyance. I'd be careful next time you light a cigarette with that device: you've put quite the cumulative charge on it.'

I glared at my lighter; then at Vadász. Grunting, I dropped it back in my pocket. 'I'll try to remember that' I grumbled, and looked out the window, trying to ascertain where we were.

'Say, Vadász—where're we headed?'

'First stop,' he said brightly, 'are the offices of *The Sun* newspaper. That being accomplished, a secondary destination will no doubt be indicated.'

I hunched back in my seat. 'Private dicks and muckrakers. I see you hang out with the best of crowds,' I snapped.

'It could be worse,' he smiled turning onto William Street.

'How so?' I bit.

'I could "hang out", as you say, with lawyers.'

* * *

We pulled up to the kerb and stepped out into the busy morning of another Sydney day. Sunlight was warming up the brickwork of the buildings lining the thoroughfare and the air reeked of coal dust and hot tar. Cars rumbled by on the blacktop accompanied by the ringing bells of trams and the tramp of feet heading to work. A few yards down from where we stood, several gulls were squabbling over something unmentionable on the footpath.

Getting into the front doors of *The Sun* offices was fraught with difficulty, mainly due to the push of newspaper men trying to rush out through the same entrance. Vadász chose his moment, then grabbed one fellow who was wrestling into his jacket while trying to operate his hat, his spiral-bound notebook between his teeth. Gripping him firmly above the elbow, Vadász neatly excised him from the departing mob and stalled him on the pavement.

'Mr Dobson,' he chirped, 'what means this explosive egress? Are the premises on fire?'

Dobson blinked a couple of times using the moment to orientate himself and get properly under his fedora. 'Mr Vadász!'

he exclaimed. 'Gee, I'd love to stop and chat, but there's a big story breaking at police headquarters.'

Vadász released him and helped straighten his lapels. 'I shan't keep you then,' he smiled, 'but can you give me the *précis*?'

Dobson's feet were already moving as he called over his shoulder, 'The police have found the missing Danvers girl! The commish is gonna hold a press conference...!' And he was gone.

'What!?' I roared. 'That's not possible! How the devil did they do that?'

'How, indeed,' Vadász muttered.

'Stay here, Vadász,' I ordered, 'I need to find a telephone.'

I rushed across the busy road to a nearby pub. Within its cool, hops-y interior, a telephone hung on the tiled wall of a corridor leading to the men's room: I summarily ejected the SP bookie who was cluttering-up the facilities and gave the number in my notebook to the exchange. It was quickly answered.

'Mr Danvers? Patrick Dolan here. I—'

'Mr Dolan,' the gravelly tones of the businessman cut me off. 'I assume you're calling because you've heard that my daughter has been recovered by the police. My wife and I have also just been informed and are about to leave for the City. No doubt you realise that this brings our mutual business to a close.'

'But—' I tried.

'Frankly, Mr Dolan,' he went on, 'it was only due to outside pressure that I sought your services at all, others whose opinions I formerly valued assuring me that leaving the business in the hands of the police would serve me ill. I believe that my faith in the constabulary has now been more than restored.'

'Until we know all the details—' I tried again.

'That will be all, Mr Dolan.' There was some fire amid all the frostiness now. 'The advance I paid in order to secure your services you may keep, and we shall call things quits. To be absolutely frank, I was suspicious of your *braggadocio* and easy assurances at first, and I find those suspicions now confirmed. All in all, I feel that, in this matter, I have been swayed in my judgement by sentiment; rest assured that it will not happen again. Good-bye, Mr Dolan, and do me the final service of losing my telephone number.' He hung up sharply.

I didn't quite break the instrument by closing the connexion at my end, but it was close.

Letting myself out onto the street once more, I saw Vadász emerging from *The Sun* offices, pulling on his gloves once more. Hunch-shouldered, my hands in my pockets, I stomped across the road towards him. I didn't particularly pay attention to the traffic: I was angry enough that, if anything had tried to run into me, I would have seriously made it regret the decision.

'So, I guess this is the end of the line for the both of us,' I grumbled as I stepped over the kerb to stand opposite him. 'Girl's found; job's done.'

He smiled serenely up at me, the slender chains around his wrists jingling faintly as he switched his cane from one hand to the other.

'Not by a long shot,' he said. 'Yes, the Danvers girl has been found, but her associate, Mr Dolan, her partner in this affair, is still very much at large.'

'Yeah, well,' I said, 'finding that feller ain't gonna pay my rent. I wasn't hired to find him, so I guess this is where we part company.'

He cocked his head at me and gave me a squinty smile. 'Mr Danvers may no longer be paying you for your time,' he said, 'but I would be more than happy for you to join your forces with mine for the time being, becoming, in effect, your client.'

I straightened up and stared down at him. 'You want me to come on board your case? Won't your backers have something to say about that?'

He smiled sideways at me as he said, 'My employers are extremely accommodating. Essentially, I have *carte blanche* to conduct things entirely as I see fit. And I could use your help, Mr Dolan.'

Given that there was potential money in his patter here, I decided to say "yes" while the offer was good. I held out my paw and he shook it gingerly.

'Alright: deal,' I said. 'Now, where do we start?'

'First,' he said, 'we find a missing girl...'

* * *

While Danvers had been telephonically kicking me in the nuts, Vadász had been doing two things at *The Sun*. First, he placed an advertisement in the "Personals" column, beseeching the intercession of St. Jude, patron saint of lost causes; and second, he read the morning edition of the newspaper. From this source he discovered that the eldest daughter of a wealthy orchardist out in the rural Wedderburn district near the small town of Appin had vanished the previous evening. Local police and concerned citizens were conducting a search even as we spoke. It appeared that she had wandered away from the homestead—a large Georgian villa set amidst an expanse of fruit trees—and was last seen heading towards the main road into Appin.

After several hours of driving, we stopped to re-fuel in Parramatta and I took the opportunity to buy a copy of the local newspaper, *The Cumberland Argus and Fruitgrowers' Advocate*. The front page screamed all the details concerning the Danvers girl, how she had wandered into police headquarters at midnight, drenched to the skin and with several broken bones; how she had no memory of the previous four days, especially of driving off in her father's Rolls Royce Silver Ghost. The reporters carried on for column inches about stultifying drugs and white slavers, all of which the police tried to downplay with terse, equivocal comments.

We turned south and entered a dry, rolling countryside, bordered further west by the Nepean River and the Blue Mountains beyond, and in every other direction by miles of nothing. Occasionally, a bedraggled cottage materialised, compiled from used wood and sheets of tin, only to fade quickly into the emptiness once more. Patches of dry eucalypts turned slowly into dense, thickets of short, green fruit trees, which in turn began to blanket the surroundings by the time a faded metal sign informed us that Appin was only a mile ahead.

Vadász threw on the brakes and the car juddered to a halt. I pulled my face out of the dent I made in the dashboard, yelling, 'Whaddaya wanna go an' do that for?!'

But he was out of the vehicle in a trice. 'Come on!' he cried, 'I've spotted something!'

I hauled my crumpled body out onto the roadside and stretched until I'd regained my accustomed dimensions. Vadász had slipped off the road and down into the gully that ran alongside it, a declivity that was overly populated by blackberries, gum trees and several stray apple saplings that had sprouted on the wrong side of the fence-line. Navigating around these impediments, he homed in on a burnt patch sheltered by a twisted eucalypt and, by the time I showed up to lend a hand, had exposed the back end of a car, ploughed headfirst into the greenery and then set alight. The canopy had been burned completely away leaving just blackened and twisted metal ribs; the tyres had melted into slag on the rims, and the paintwork was a crackled mess.

Vadász crouched down and pulled—to my surprise—a flick-knife from his pocket. He gently scratched at the ash obscuring the maker's medallion on the boot panel. Then, 'It's a Roller,' he said, standing and trousering the blade, 'Silver Ghost, or I miss my mark.'

He scrambled back up the slope to our wheels. I scratched my head, then followed, the cogs in my brain manoeuvring into a higher gear.

'Alright,' I said squeezing back into the Oldsmobile, 'so it's a wrecked Rolls Royce. It's a damned shame, but so what?'

Vadász was drumming his fingers on the wheel, eager to be away.

'It's not *a* Rolls Royce Silver Ghost,' he said, wrenching the car into gear and pulling sharply out onto the road once more, 'it's *the* Rolls Royce Silver Ghost. The one that belongs to Danvers.'

'What?' My cogs began to mesh uncomfortably. 'What would Danvers' car be doing all the way out here in whoop-whoop?'

'When we find the missing girl, you'll have your answer,' he grinned.

My head was spinning. 'But the missing girl is no longer missing,' I complained, 'the police have her.'

'The police have Grace Danvers; ergo, she's no longer unaccounted-for,' he corrected me. 'We're looking for a *missing* girl, remember?'

'I don't see what the one has to do with the other,' I whinged.

'That's because you're still working on a field that's far too small for the game we're playing. Look—we're here at Appin. Let's talk to the local police.'

* * *

It had taken us all day to drive to this outpost. Appin was a small town, a speck in the midst of wide-spreading fruit orchards—two hotels, a post office, police station, municipal council buildings and a petrol station. The day was gaspingly hot, and I had shucked my coat and jacket, more comfortable in shirt sleeves and vest. Even Vadász had shed his coat. The afternoon sky was red, populated with pink-tinged clouds. Billows of dust blew through the town centre from off the parched rolling hills around us.

As we pushed through the door into the police station, we observed a senior officer to one side in the foyer holding court with a trio of reporters, outlining the circumstances of the vanished girl. To my surprise, Vadász strode across to the desk sergeant and shook his hand.

'Hey, Vadász!' I said, gesturing towards the reporters: surely, he couldn't be that obtuse?

Nevertheless, he addressed the jack at the desk. 'I wonder if you could tell me if there have been any reports of a stolen car in town within the last, say, twelve hours?'

The sergeant, obviously expecting questions about the biggest current news item in town, did a double-take and all but let his jaw land on the blotter. Fixing Vadász with boggle-eyes, he flipped a page backwards in his ledger. His inky finger ran down a few lines of cramped scrawl before stopping.

'Well, yes,' he said, 'Mr Larcombe's 1923 Peugeot Torpedo Sport was stolen out of his garage last night.'

'And this Mr Larcombe would be...?' Vadász asked.

'He owns *Larcombe's Fruit Salts*. Here in Appin.'

'Ah, of course: I thought the name sounded familiar. Any further details you can give me?'

'Well,' the sergeant hunched forward, 'the report suggests that whoever took the car used a tractor to pull the doors off the garage...'

'A tractor?'

'Yes, indeed. The doors were pulled right out of the frame.'

'Really?' Vadász inclined towards his oracle. 'And tell me—did anyone see which way the car went afterwards?'

'Yes,' said the sergeant, 'an officer coming in to work saw the car headed south out of town. He didn't attach any importance to it at the time, though.'

'Excellent!' Vadász cried. 'Many thanks sergeant—you've been very helpful.' He pushed away from the desk and headed quickly for the door. Incredulous, I spun in his wake, watching him exit. The desk sergeant cleared his throat behind me.

'Are you sure you fellers aren't interested in the Hope McAllister disappearance?' he asked.

'Mate,' I said, 'when I know what's going on myself, you'll be the first person I tell.'

I trudged heavily after Vadász, hauling out my cigarettes as I did so.

The burst of flame from my lighter almost took my eyebrows off.

* * *

Heading south, the roads got—if anything—even worse as the sun descended. I hunched over in my seat, wrestling with a map and a dodgy torch, trying to navigate the way forward. A short stop at a remote petrol station, where we prevented the attendant from closing for the night, gave us a lucky break: he'd topped-up a car like the one we were following, driven by a young brunette. She'd asked him about the best route out to the coast and he'd given her some very detailed directions east, towards Wollongong. We set off again, using that same advice.

As we rumbled and jerked through the night on the roughest of dirt tracks, our headlamps picking out roadside eucalypts like startled ghosts, I tried to make sense of things by bearding the sphinx in his den.

'Alright, so we're interested in Hope McAllister now?' I posited.

'Indeed,' answered Vadász.

'And therefore, we're not just tracking down a stolen car?'

Vadász chuckled. 'Mr Dolan, has it not occurred to you that we're doing both? Hope McAllister is the young woman in the stolen vehicle.'

'That's clear,' I nodded, 'but how could she have organised the theft? I mean, someone got a tractor to tear the garage doors off and get the car. Could Hope have organised all of that?'

'I don't think you're giving her the credit she deserves,' he said, 'but no, I think she tore them from the hinges with her bare hands.'

I goggled at him. 'You're not serious?'

'I'm always serious,' he smiled, 'despite my sunny demeanour.'

'But even *I* couldn't do that, and I'm plenty hefty.'

Vadász waved a dismissive hand. 'Put that fact aside in your mind for now and think about other elements of the puzzle. For instance, what connects Grace Danvers and Hope McAllister?'

'Not a damned thing,' I insisted.

He fired a sly, sidelong smile at me. 'Are you sure? You don't think the fact that they're both seventeen and have unfeasibly difficult names to live up to is at all interesting?'

I frowned at him. 'Coincidence.'

'In my line of work, things are rarely ever that simple. Young women of good standing and fast, expensive cars—tell me you don't see a pattern at work here?'

My brain hurt. 'Alright, so there's a pattern. A coincidental one, that's all I'll concede, but yes, a pattern. What I don't see is why. Or how.'

'Those will come later,' he stared out at the road, his mouth a thin, set line. 'For now, it's enough that you've taken the first step into a wider world.'

* * *

By dawn, after changing a flat tyre, we had passed through Thirroul and Bulli and were rolling through lush, fern-encrusted forest down into Wollongong. The town spread out before and below us, forming a bulkhead between the bush and the sea. The Pacific Ocean pulsed blackly in the grey light, sparkled intermittently by the beam of a lighthouse sweeping across it from the breakwater that curled northwards from the low, sea-ringed mound of Wollongong Head. We were soon riding through straggling homes which grew in number to become suburbs and then the city centre—such as it was.

We stopped outside the Town Hall as the eastern horizon went from a pale fish-belly shimmer to a scorching orange. I unfolded myself from the car with a groan, stretching luxuriantly after the long, cramped drive.

'Now, if we can just find breakfast somewhere around here,' I said, 'that would be perfect.'

However, Vadász was staring out to sea, towards the breakwater and the Head beside it. The harbour entrance was busy with trawlers returning from a night on the open sea and gulls mounted the morning salt-breezes, cackling their mournful cries.

'What do you see out there?' he said to me, pointing.

'Boats. Water. Birds.' I summed up.

'Take this,' he said, pulling a small brass telescope out of his coat pocket. 'Look at the end of the breakwater, near the base of that promontory.'

Grunting, I extended the spyglass and trained it to where he'd indicated. Within its crystal circumference, I saw distant waves smashing against the stone barrier, white spume flying into the air and cascading down onto a parked Peugeot Torpedo Sport.

I jerked my head back from the eyepiece. 'Is that it?' I asked.

Vadász was skipping back to the Oldsmobile. 'I assume so,' he said, 'and, if we're lucky, the girl won't be too far away.'

The drive was a matter of minutes, despite the car complaining about its overuse. We pulled up behind the Peugeot, noticing that it had been crashed through a barrier erected specifically to deter such an intrusion. The driver's side door hung open and the radiator was cracked and had emptied copiously. I stuck my head inside to examine the vehicle's interior but withdrew it immediately, gagging and choking.

'*Christ!*' I coughed. 'It stinks in there! What is that?'

'Oh, rot; decay; sulphur,' Vadász was seemingly unaffected, giving the car a cursory once-over, 'the usual.' He turned as the wan beam from the lighthouse sheened over us. 'There,' he said, pointing up to the Head: 'that's where she'll be. Come on—I believe I saw a road back there which will take us up to the top.'

Back in the Oldsmobile, we re-traced our route a little and took a left-hand fork which lifted us steadily to the top of the wide, rocky promontory, crowned with wind-tossed grass. As we got closer, I could feel the tension coming off Vadász like waves of electricity: he knew we were getting closer and his excitement was palpable.

The road became a wide circle topping the Head and allowing a panoramic view out to the sea on all sides save the landward one. As we rounded the monumental flagpole which topped the eminence, the figure of a young girl with dark hair swung into view, barefoot in a plain print dress. Vadász swung the car off the road and drove across the grass towards her.

He slammed on the brakes when we were about twenty feet away.

'Come on, Vadász!' I yelled, catching something of his excitement, 'get closer or she'll give us the slip!'

'No, Dolan,' he answered, shutting off the engine, 'this is safe enough.'

'Safe?' I was bewildered. 'It's not like she's dangerous!'

'Appearances are deceiving, Mr Dolan,' he said, stepping out onto the grass, 'you don't want to be knocked out by a seventeen-year-old girl twice in two days, do you?' He grabbed the thermos and one of the books from inside the car and stuffed them in his coat pockets before moving over towards her; grumbling, I stepped out of the vehicle and followed suit.

We approached cautiously—although for what reason I couldn't discern—from behind her. I followed Vadász's lead, walking softly, tensed and ready, keeping quiet. She stood looking out to sea, the far horizon a blushing backdrop before her. Her hair was unbound and swung about her shoulders in the salt breeze. Her skin was bluish-pale and marred by the dark smudging of bruises.

'Anton Vadász,' a voice boomed out, 'you are beginning to seriously annoy me.'

I stopped sharply and looked around me, scanning the surroundings for a hidden fourth person. The voice was loud and deep, the deepest voice I think I've ever heard. I'd read about voices booming in novels before but, after hearing this utterance, I had a benchmark for exactly what that expression meant.

'Then obviously,' responded Vadász, 'I'm obtaining satisfactory results.'

There was a hissing sound, loud and thrilling, something between an agitated snake-pit and a bucket of nails being tipped down a tin roof. A cold finger of ice lanced down my spine and my knees turned suddenly to water. With that sound, the girl turned to face us.

To say that her appearance shocked me would be an understatement. Her eyes had rolled back into her head, showing stark white and ringed by heavy blue-black shadows; veins stood out across her forehead and neck, and her pale lips parted to reveal yellowed teeth and a lolling greenish-grey tongue. Her head rolled upon her neck as if she was having difficulty supporting it. The reek that had permeated the Peugeot bubbled tenfold in her vicinity. I broke out in a cold sweat and my heart fluttered like I'd just run fifty yards down a football pitch to score a try.

'*Fool!*' the voice boomed again, and the sound of it seemed to come from all around us, despite the fact that her lips clearly framed the word. 'You think you have found me; you have found only—*your death!*'

A hot wind burst in upon us. Vadász leapt in front of me and raised both fists before his face, crossed at the wrists, his chains with all their pendant medallions and charms shining in the early light. From my vantage point over the top of his homburg, I saw the girl's head loll in the other direction and her blank-eyed face took on the expression of a cat examining a newly broken parrot.

The wind stopped as suddenly as it had begun; the air around us felt dense and silent. I saw a faint orange trickle next to the girl's left ear and another flowed upwards along her jawline. A myriad more flickered into view around her like a halo of floating candle flames.

With a hideous snarl, she suddenly thrust out a bruised arm at us. From her outstretched hand, a torrent of flame flowed forth. A storm of fire crashed into Vadász as all the interrupted noise of the world fell upon us once more...

I think I blacked out temporarily. Next thing I knew, I heard Vadász calling out to me: 'Dolan? Mr Dolan—are you alright?'

I was lying on the grass staring up at him; he was looking down at me over his left shoulder, his arms still crossed at the wrists. His gloves were singed and the chains around his forearms were glowing red, slowly fading.

'Am I alright? What about you?'

Another burst of flame washed over us. Vadász fell down, screaming, on top of me. In the aftermath, we were coughing and choking.

'*Run!*' cried Vadász.

'Your trinkets won't help you for much longer,' the voice hissed out, like the mother of all rattlesnakes. 'I feel them weakening—soon your armour will break.'

'Get to the car!' Vadász urged me. I didn't need to be told twice. I scrabbled to my unsteady feet and careened drunkenly towards the Oldsmobile, my arms cartwheeling wildly. As I rounded the boot-end, I heard the roar of flames again and looked back to see Vadász once more deflect its power, as if there were a glass barrier between him and the girl. If barrier it was, however, it was beginning to fail and Vadász spun around to crash into the car with the sleeve of his coat on fire.

'Mr Dolan,' he gasped, smacking the flames out with his gloved hand, 'how are you at throwing things?'

'Pretty good,' I answered, 'you got a grenade or something we can toss at this...thing?'

He shook his head wearily. Keeping one eye on the girl as she slowly stepped nearer, he pulled something out of his coat pocket and slammed it on the car roof, extending it as far as he could towards me. 'Please, would you throw this at her?' he said.

Trying to keep my head down, I lunged for the proffered object and ducked once more.

'Vadász,' I called out, 'this is a thermos. What—are you going to give her a cup of tea?'

'Please just try to hit her with it,' he called back, gasping, 'we don't have much time.'

I hefted the thermos and heard a rustling sound within it. Obviously, the glass bottle inside had shattered and whatever it contained was now laced with glass shards. I hoped that fact made little difference to Vadász's plan. Standing up quickly, I sighted my target, who was now disturbingly closer than I felt comfortable with and winding up for another gout of fire. I hauled back and chucked the thermos like everything depended upon it.

Her head snapped up as the bottle soared over the vehicle towards her. Almost negligently, she flicked a fiery hand at it and turned her basilisk gaze back upon Vadász.

The thermos burst into pure, yellow-white fire and rained down on her amid a shower of silvered glass fragments and enamelled tin. She screamed, and the sound of it left me curled up on the grass beside the car. It was a sound that cut straight through a person and struck the middle of who you were: it was utterly terrible and there was no defence against it.

Someone grabbed my arm and started pulling. 'Well done, Mr Dolan,' Vadász congratulated me, 'but we're not finished yet.'

He'd flung open the passenger side door of the Oldsmobile and scrabbled through to the other side of the car leaving the doors hanging open like useless wings. He hauled me up while trying to keep his head lowered, darting occasional glances through the rear windows towards our quarry.

'What the hell was in that?' I yelled, getting to my knees.

Vadász gave me a glance. His coat was scorched and some of his hair was singed; his gloves were tattered and the chains around his wrists hung in disarray, some of them turned to molten slag. 'Holy oil,' he said, with a quick smile, 'a gift from a Greek Orthodox priest of my acquaintance.'

'You got any more?'

'No,' he answered with a rueful smile, 'it's not that easy to come by.'

I looked through the car's rear windows to see what the girl was doing. Our attack had obviously had an impact: all her hair, clothing and skin had burned away, and she was wreathed in a dying veil of fire. As I stared, she threw back her head and revealed a terrible visage of blistered flesh and scorched bone. Despite this, her eyeless sockets stared towards us with a steady malevolence as—incredibly—she staggered to her feet once more. Sickened, I began to turn away, but something made me stop and look again.

As I watched, the burnt jaw worked, chewing the air, and soon a tongue moved in the charred mouth; the empty sockets bubbled and twitched then blinked, and when they opened, the evil eyes were restored once more. Bit by bit, she started to re-grow herself from her burnt ruin.

'*God damn it!*' I spat ducking down behind the car once more. 'Wasn't that enough?'

'Language, Mr Dolan, and no, not nearly,' said Vadász. He winced as he pulled a melted chain out of the skin of his hand. He rattled what was left of the little rock crystal jar it had held. 'A relic of St. Lawrence,' he said. 'That wasn't easy to find.'

'Well, what's next?' I growled, 'she's not going away.'

Vadász pulled a leather book out of his coat pocket. 'We do this the hard way,' he said. There was a steely look in his eyes; his sunny demeanour had gone. 'There's a kerosene tin full of holy water in the back seat,' he said, 'when I start reading, get it out and get ready to drench her with it.'

He stood up quickly and deftly flicked the book open with an easy movement borne of long familiarity. He began reading loudly, words I recognised from my Catholic upbringing but nothing I understood. I grabbed the handle for the Oldsmobile's back door and began to open it. Sudden chilling laughter made me stop.

'Remigius?' the evil voice boomed forth again. 'You can't be serious, Vadász. *The Daemonolatreia* is a fraud—didn't you know? How delicious!'

Vadász stammered to a halt. 'It's worked before,' he said, 'very effectively...'

The girl cut him off. 'Yes, against lesser imps and incursions of a minor sort. If it had no value at all, Remigius would never have traded his soul for it, much less published the thing. It had to have enough truth to convince him, but no real power. Your weapons are useless, Vadász; it's time you accepted the fact.' She raised her arms and the bright flickering flames danced around her again.

Vadász stared down at his book and then back at her, his mouth working like a hooked fish. Around us, the pressure increased as she got ready to drench us with fire once more.

'Bugger this for a game of soldiers,' I said.

Taking a deep breath, I jumped to my feet and darted out from behind the car, rounding the boot and dodging towards what was left of Hope McAllister. Using all the strength I could muster, I kept low and barrelled straight into her, crash-tackling her into the car's open door with a squeal of hinges. Grabbing her as tightly as I could, I rolled over and vaulted into the passenger seat, falling on top of her and pinning her down with my bulk.

'Fool!' she hissed, 'now you burn!'

Despite myself, my heart was trip-hammering again and I shut my eyes, gritting my teeth as the car's interior flooded with pulsing orange light...

'Well done, Mr Dolan,' Vadász's voice rolled in through the driver's door, 'Just keep her there if you would.'

'What? What is this?' The girl struggled and bucked beneath me, and I realised that I had my work cut out for me trying to hold her in place.

She glared, blank-eyed at me and the orange lines and sigils that covered the Oldsmobile's interior pulsed luridly several times more.

'The car,' I said through gritted teeth, 'resists fire. You're just wasting your time.' At that point, Vadász slapped me in the face with a gush of holy water.

If she was struggling before, now she went completely wild. I grabbed her wrists; she kneed me in the groin. I punched her in the jaw; she bit my hand. Then I really lost my temper...

The red haze lowered as I was ejected from the car, landing flat on the grass with the wind knocked out of me. I looked up in time to see the girl's head bent back and a horrid black smoke pouring out of her nose and mouth. The dark cloud swirled about her, slowly hiding her from view, then sped out and into the bright morning air. As it did so, it flickered once with flame then burst in the biggest incendiary explosion I'd ever seen...

* * *

Later, Vadász and I leant against the car sharing my last cigarette. His face and hands were reddened and blistered, and his hat had disappeared; I had a black eye, swollen closed, and my face was scratched seven ways from Sunday. About us, sea and sky were baby-blue, dotted respectively with idle clouds and bobbing boats. In the back seat of the Oldsmobile, Hope McAllister slept the sleep of the innocent, in our borrowed coats and an old picnic blanket that Vadász conjured up from somewhere.

'So: possessed, huh?' I said, handing the cigarette over with skinned-knuckle fingers. 'I thought that kind of thing only happened in medieval French nunneries.'

Vadász took a drag and let the smoke slowly escape through his broken nose. 'Sadly no,' he said, 'it's actually more common than you'd think. Not usually this bad, though.'

I snorted, accepting the smoke back. 'I guess we can be grateful for small mercies. You don't really have any backers, do you?'

He winced, then smiled. 'Not of the sort you mean, Mr Dolan. I have my own finances and connexions to various—interested—organisations and personages.'

'I can guess,' I said.

He took the cigarette back and took a last draw from it before flicking it off into the grass. 'What interests me,' he said, 'is how you were able to keep her pinned down in there. Strong as you are, I've seen lesser entities deal easily with greater forces arrayed against them.'

I smirked. 'You can thank Brother Joseph for that, I reckon,' I said. 'As kids, he would flay our hides if we left the dormitory without our scapulars on. It's a habit that I've never really gotten out of.' I pulled open my shirt and revealed the Catholic talisman tied against my chest, with the words *"Whosoever dies wearing this Scapular shall not suffer Eternal Fire"* embroidered in gold thread. 'I guess you're not the only one carrying protective trinkets.'

Vadász laughed merrily. 'Patrick, you are a miracle!' he chuckled and broke off, coughing.

'No, Anton,' I countered, 'a miracle would be breakfast, appearing right now before us on gold plates and a linen tablecloth.'

We spent a moment looking upwards into the benign blue sky, but nothing happened.

'Well, it was worth a shot,' I said. 'Let's get back to Sydney...'

Matthew Hopkins Witch Finder Generall
My Imps names are
1 Ilemauzar
2 Pywackett
Jarmara
3 Pecke in the Crowne
4 Griezzell Greedigutt
Sacke & Sugar
Newes
Vinegar Tom

II.

"HAVOC!"

HAVOC

"CRY 'HAVOC!' AND LET SLIP THE DOGS OF WAR..."

**_-MARK ANTONY, JULIUS CAESAR, ACT 3, SCENE 1,
LINE 273_**

I'm not a person who's inclined towards waiting. I get fidgety. When I get fidgety, I get cranky, and that's when I'm liable to break something.

The guy I was chasing was out there somewhere, and I had no means of being able to follow him. All I could do was try and get in front of him somehow, to anticipate where he might turn up and cut him off before he did any more damage.

Black shadows striped the front room of the house that I was in, thrown by the porch lights across the street, cutting in through the Venetian blinds. Outside, the road gleamed from a recent fall of rain and thunder rumbling overhead told of more to come. The humidity had risen to a stifling degree and I had shrugged out of my jacket to lessen its effects.

The house I was glaring at across the way was not a nice place. It looked like any run-of-the-mill, two-up two-down Paddington terrace, but it was actually one of the many *bordellos* that throve in this district, hiding cheek-by-jowl with legitimate homes and businesses. Women and cocaine were to be had on the premises, sometimes both together, along with a hefty helping of sly grog. The owner would be paying a heaping proportion of their takings to Kate Leigh or Tilly Devine, or even both, depending upon where the illegal boundaries of territory were drawn.

The fellow I was waiting for was certain to show up here at some point: his desperation deemed it so. The proprietress of the whorehouse—one Nancy Coombes—was a shrewd businesswoman, one who carried on her work while keeping her head below the parapets. She had a record with the jacks, of course, and had even done some time in gaol, but it was unlikely that she would get caught a second time. She had taken the measure of the market and she knew how to conduct herself and her trade. She was hard-headed and canny; she was also my mark's sister.

Odds were that he would show up here for help, sooner rather than later. My main problem was that when he did, I would have trouble spotting him. The last time I'd clapped eyes on him, earlier this evening, he was a burnt-out husk, blackened and roasted on the floor of a slum-land hovel. Not that something like that would slow him down.

Across the street, the front door opened, and a figure stepped out. It was a man, dressed in a shabby suit and tie, his face obscured by the shadows thrown by his fedora. He leaned out over the railing of the terrace patio and looked up and down the street. Then, he leant back against the wall next to the front door and began to roll himself a cigarette. I watched him until a tram rattled past and cut him off from view.

'Tea, Patrick?'

I glanced sideways. There was a nun leaning over the back of the couch I was sitting on, handing me a rose-painted cup and saucer, steaming with the beverage.

'Thanks, Bea,' I said, gratefully reaching for the drink.

'Uh-uh,' she countered, 'Sister Immaculata, remember?'

I winced. 'Sure,' I said. 'Sorry—I can't get used to the name-change.'

A lifetime ago, Bea used to be one of my many cousins, children of my mum's sister Deirdre, whose husband had died in the Great War. Her brother Terry and I used to tear around the streets with our gang of friends, raising Hell, with little Beatrice always bringing up the rear. When I'd realised that my quarry was going to be across the street from her old place, I tracked her down. You can imagine my surprise when I learned that she'd taken vows.

She lifted her veil and flapped it gently, waving a hand to draw fresh air across her neck.

'Phew!' she said, 'this heat: really wears you down, doesn't it?'

I looked at her again. 'Do you have to wear that penguin suit all the time?' I asked.

She nodded. 'Pretty much; 'comes with the territory.'

I stuck a finger down my collar and ran it around a bit, trying to loosen it a little. I slurped my tea. It wasn't as hot as I usually like, but it hit the spot.

Bea moved around the couch to perch on the armrest furthest from me. She squinted forwards through the round lenses of her spectacles, out towards the terrace opposite.

'Do you think he'll show up tonight?' she asked.

I put my teacup down on a small table next to me, careful to use the coaster which I'm sure wasn't there by accident.

'He doesn't have a lot of options,' I said. 'He's in a jam and his sister is probably the only one who has any idea about how to get him out of it.'

'It's odd,' she said after a slight pause, 'to think that something like this is happening over there, just across the street.'

'It's odd to think of stuff like this happening at all,' I scoffed. 'One year ago, if you told me this was going on, I'd've laughed in your face, nun or no nun.'

She smiled over at me through the barred darkness.

'I see we've had an epiphany,' she smiled.

'Definitely a "Road to Damascus" moment,' I said, 'although, more like a road to Wollongong...'

'And this fellow you work with—Anton Vadász,' she said, 'is he a believer too?'

'I'm pretty sure,' I replied, 'although I think narrowing down his beliefs would be fairly tricky—he's sort of open to everything.'

'He comes with a strong endorsement from Father Thomas,' she observed.

'Yeah, and Father Miklos from the Greek Orthodox crowd. And then there's Ji Daoyi down in Chinatown...'

'Stop!' insisted Bea, raising a hand, 'I don't need to know any more. If Father Thomas gives him the nod, that's enough for me. But how are *you* juggling all of this?'

I waved a dismissive hand. I craned my neck to look quickly around the room.

'Why haven't you sold this place, Bea?' I asked.

'Not mine to sell,' she answered. 'I gave up my share when I became a nun; Terry owns it now. But I still have a key.'

'Lucky for me,' I said. I looked around once more. 'You know, your mum was really proud of this front room. We would get in so much trouble if we ran through here, or tracked in any muck…'

'Yes,' said Bea, 'she always kept this room "for best". The rest of the place could fall into ruin—which it never did—but this room had to be spotless. It was the front that she presented to the world.'

'Who lives here now?'

Bea sighed and brushed the nap of the couch fabric. 'No-one,' she said. 'Terry sometimes stays here if he's in Town. He'd probably try to sell it though, if he knew the sort of things that are happening in the neighbourhood.' Here, she nodded across the road.

'Fair enough,' I said. 'You know anything about this Nancy Coombes?'

'Only what I read in the papers, and that's very little. She keeps thing very quiet. The only time she really appears is if one of her henchmen needs someone to post bail for them.'

'Guys like that one playing cockatoo over there, keeping an eye out for trouble. How many thugs does she have on the payroll?'

Bea looked at me sideways. 'Patrick, I haven't a clue—I'm just a nun with special dispensation to spend time away from my hospital duties due to "family issues". I know very little about this woman.'

'Yeah, sorry,' I said, 'it's just that not knowing makes me nervous.'

'Well, keep watching. I'll make us some more tea.'

There was a loud clanging sound as another tram rattled by in the night, sparks showering down from the cable above. A bored conductor leaned against a brass rail, yawning hugely as he slid by into darkness. When it had gone, the scene across the road had changed and I sat up, craning forward.

A kid stood on the pavement, hatless and dishevelled, his attitude one of pleading. The guard on the front door was staring down at him from the three-step height of the front porch, his hand creeping past the left lapel of his coat. I couldn't hear what was being said, but it was clear from the sneer on the guy's physog that he wasn't impressed with the visitor. He pointed at the fellow's shoes, a gesture meaning "stay put", and then turned to knock sharply on the front door. It cracked open after a minute or so—I shifted about, trying to see who was answering but to no avail. Suddenly, it swung wide and Nancy Coombes stood there in all her poisonous glory.

She was tall and statuesque, dressed in a house frock like butter wouldn't melt. She wore a cairngorm brooch and a diamante watch and she was made up like it was Sunday to church. Her hair was coiffed, pulled back into a neat bun from the stark widow's peak of her hairline and her eyebrows arched like two villainous parabolas beneath. The frosty mask of her features could freeze water at ten paces. She spoke to the cringing visitor, just a couple of sentences, and then stepped back inside, signalling him to follow after her. He lolloped up the stairs like a grateful puppy.

'Any luck?' said Bea walking back into the room behind me.

'We're up,' I said, adjusting my collar and reaching for my hat. When I turned to her, she was standing with a cup of tea on a saucer, looking at me. I reached for it and downed it in one swallow—I guess nuns don't know how to make hot tea.

'Look,' I said, placing the cup back on the saucer in her hands, 'I'm not sure how this is going to turn out, but it could get messy. Are you on the telephone here?'

She nodded quickly.

'Alright. Be ready to call for help if you think it necessary. Or if I don't come back before sun-up. Father Thomas will know how to contact Anton.'

I shrugged into my jacket.

'Wish me luck!' I said.

'I'll pray for you,' she said, her hands carefully enfolding the teacup. I slipped out into the cloying dark...

* * *

The fellow on guard was lighting a cigarette as I stealthily approached. He threw back his head, inhaling, then flipped the match out into the street. I caught it and flicked it back at him, letting it ricochet off the light fixture to the left of the door. Like an idiot, he looked at the light then bent closer to examine it minutely. That made it easy for me to grab him by the back of the head and smack his forehead into the brickwork. He went down like a sack of swedes.

I laid him out on the porch and reached into his coat. Pulling out the pistol he had hidden there, I made sure the safety was on and chucked it across the street. Then I propped him up against the wall and crossed his legs at the ankles: after tipping his hat down over his face, you couldn't have said that he was anything other than a mug sleeping off a heavy night.

I tried the doorknob tentatively. To my surprise, it wasn't locked. Timing my movements with another passing tram, I opened the door and slipped inside...

The tram lights through the windows swept the room. In front of me was a set of stairs headed upwards; to my left a doorway opened on a room with a couch and armchairs. Before me to the left of the stairs was a passageway headed deeper into the dark. There were lights on above and small sounds of movement; light gleamed around the edges of a door at the end of the dark passage. I decided I'd better check what was down there before taking the high road.

As I took a step towards the back of the house, a low rumbling growl made me stop suddenly. A strong reek of something noxious billowed over me. I fumbled for my lighter and snapped it on, trying to throw light on the midnight corridor.

Lying on the hall rug in front of me was a big dog. I knew it was big because, even though it was curled up, it still touched the skirting boards on either side. It was a big Bull Terrier from what I could make out: it had that same sloping, no-frills, nothing-to-grab-onto-shaped head. I'd never seen one that was completely black before. Or one whose eyes glowed red, like hot coals.

'Easy boy,' I soothed.

In response, it lifted its head and growled once more. Its teeth were so big that a penny wouldn't have covered one of them, and flames flickered out between them. A plume of dark smoke billowed out of the side of its mouth. A voice broke the silence from above.

'It's a Hellhound,' said Nancy and took a drag on a cigarette, 'it won't do anything unless you do something stupid. You won't do anything *stupid*, will you?'

I snapped off my lighter.

'I guess not,' I said.

'Then come upstairs,' she said, 'I suppose we should talk business.'

I took a slow step backwards and manoeuvred the newel post of the banister between me and the mutt. It grunted in a disappointed kind of way and dropped its head back onto its paws, but its glowing eyes tracked every movement I made as I trudged slowly up the stairs...

* * *

Thunder rumbled as Nancy led the way through a door at the head of the stairway. She stood against the far wall while I entered the room, smoking thoughtfully and giving me an appraising stare. As her gaze narrowed, she idly flicked ash onto the carpet. I had a sense that, had I been a Neenish tart, there would have been very little holding her back.

The room appeared to be a kind of office: a large desk and captain's chair facing a pair of glazed doors that let out to an upper storey balcony, a couple of filing cabinets and a potted palm trying not to blend in with the patterned wallpaper. Outside, it began to rain in a heavy, desultory kind of way.

'Sit,' Nancy ordered, indicating an antimacassared armchair in the corner. She perched briskly in the desk chair and spun around to face me once I'd complied.

'How tall would you say you are?' She threw the question at me apropos of nothing.

'Sorry?' I answered.

'In your socks,' she continued.

I reached carefully towards my jacket pocket. 'You mind if I smoke?' I asked.

'Slowly,' she answered, eyes slitting. 'It takes Vinegar Tom only a second to get up here from down below.'

I pulled out my cigarettes and lighter and lit up, careful to leave my *accoutrements* balanced on the chair's arm afterwards, in plain sight.

'"Vinegar Tom", huh?' I said, blowing smoke, 'that the dog's name?'

'Yes,' she said, smiling, 'he's *quite* famous.'

'Six-eight,' I said settling into my chair. 'In my socks.'

'Well, well,' she purred, 'quite the man-mountain, aren't we?'

'I get by.' I looked around for an ashtray. I didn't want both of us acting like Philistines. She turned, grabbed something from the desktop, then held out a silver tray in my direction, like one of those fancy rectangular plates that the mail, or visiting cards, get delivered on, usually by the butler. I grunted and took it from her, putting my smokes and lighter on one end of it and placing it on the chair's arm. I gingerly tapped the ash off my cigarette onto it.

I craned my neck as if listening. 'Slow night?' I asked, 'pretty quiet up here.'

She blew a plume of smoke out of the side of her mouth. The nails of the thumb and pinkie finger of the hand which held her cigarette clicked together manically.

'It's a family night,' she said, 'we lock the girls away for the evening and Danny turns the punters away at the door.'

'So, what—you barricade them in their rooms with their rations of cocaine, huh? Leave 'em to it?'

'Oh, nothing so tawdry,' she replied waving her hand, 'our girls aren't snowdroppers or boozehounds—they're altogether far better behaved.'

'This him?' The voice came from the doorway. A young man stood there, maybe seventeen years of age, slight of frame and tow-headed. He was bare foot, in trousers and a fresh shirt, struggling into his braces. His hair had been oiled and combed and he reeked of soap.

'I believe he's the one,' Nancy replied, standing up. I stood up slowly too.

'This is my brother Maury,' she said to me with a casual gesture, 'I don't believe we caught your name...?'

'I don't believe I lobbed it at you,' I answered.

'Oh, he's *perfect!*' Maury padded over towards me patting his fingertips together in an acquisitive fashion. I took in his wide-eyed gaze staring up at me and moved back as far as the chair behind me would allow.

'I'm good,' I growled, 'but I ain't *that* good.' His proximity was causing me some discomfort.

'Oh yes,' Maury went on, 'he'll do *fine...*'

He reached a pale hand towards me. I tensed ready for anything, but he suddenly stopped. A spasm crossed his face and turned it instantly into a mask of barely controlled anger.

'*He's got something on him!*' he screamed, whipping around to his sister. She looked at him, startled, then ran her gaze over me. Maury turned on her, continuing his demented rant. I noticed that Nancy backed quickly away from his approach, bumping into the edge of the desk.

'*Why the Hell would you bring it here if you knew it was warded?!*' he screamed. '*Are you stupid?!*'

'Calm *down*, Maury,' Nancy soothed, raising her hands; but to calm him or keep him away, I'm sure neither of us could be certain. 'I'll *deal* with it.'

'*You better, you bitch!*' Maury's face was apoplectic, bright red with veins cording his brow. As Nancy slid passed him, he ran both his hands over his face, tearing at his skin and grimacing like a maniac. '*I refuse to stay like this!*'

Nancy leaned in close to me, pushing aside my jacket and tie in frantic jerks and running her nails over my shirt. She was no longer the cool businesswoman; her eyes were radiating a barely controlled panic.

'H-he's wearing a phylactery,' she said suddenly, with a burst of panicked laughter, 'it's not a problem: I'll just get rid of it...'

I grabbed both her hands by the wrists and raised them upwards. 'You can try,' I snarled. She gasped and her eyes went wide, filled with fear and... pleading? Behind her, I heard a chuckle from Maury.

'Oh, very *good*,' he said menacingly. He'd gained some semblance of control over himself, but his eyes still said "madman" to everyone in the vicinity. 'You *know* how this works, don't you?' he said, prowling over towards us.

'Enlighten me,' I growled.

'I touch someone; I *become* them. It's *that* easy,' he said. 'But this freedom only lasts until dawn and I certainly don't want to be in *this* body when the sun rises—it's too sickly and pathetic. But I *like* the cut of your jib, let me tell you...'

'I don't know,' I snapped back, 'that kid's probably got more years left in him than I have, and probably a better liver to boot.'

'Your Catholic bauble might make things a little tricky for me to take over your body at first, but I'm certain to succeed in the end, regardless...'

'You can try mate, but you'll have to go through your sister to get to me,' I snarled. Nancy whimpered.

'But you see, that's the *plan.*' He walked up behind Nancy wiggling his fingers. 'I touch *Nancy*; I take *her* over. She's touching *you*; I then take *you* over. Like passing from one train carriage to the next. That leaves these two bodies empty and occupant-free, but I get what I want in the end.'

He leaned close and purred in his sister's ear. 'You won't mind working with the other girls now, will you Nancy?'

With a desperate cry, she wrenched a hand free from my grasp and grabbed at my phylactery through my shirt. With a sharp tug she tore the talisman free, ripping it away from my chest, along with a sizable piece of fabric. She wheeled away sideways, cringing away from Maury's proximity and washed up, gasping, against the filing cabinets. Buttons pinged off the wallpaper.

'Attagirl,' said Maury and took a step closer to me, extending a hand. I raised my fists, not at all sure that anything I could do was going to have an effect...

'Excuse me,' came a polite, accented voice from the doorway, 'I hope I am interrupting something? Yes?'

Maury and Nancy both spun around, long lives with guilty consciences making them flinch when caught by unsuspected parties.

'*Anton!*' I gasped. 'About bloody time you showed up!'

'Sorry,' he said, brushing raindrops off his jacket, his bracelet charms jingling, 'there was a guard downstairs, so I had to resort to a downspout and a back window.' He winced: 'I'm afraid I may have caught my trouser leg on a nail...'

At that point, Maury screamed and slapped his hand on my chest.

Initially, my heart sunk; but then, there was a burst of blue-white light and Maury flew back, his hand sizzling. Anton neatly sidestepped the careening, borrowed body and slid over to me along the wall, where I stood in amazement, glowing all over with a fading, faint blue light.

'What in Hell...?' I said.

'Quite remarkable,' Anton said in a rush, 'here: take this. We're about to have company.'

He shoved a tapered piece of rusted metal into my hand: in my fist its point projected about an inch from one side and the flattened end stood proud above my thumb.

'Wha—?' I managed. Anton grabbed my arm and shook me.

'*Use* it,' he said sternly, pointing; 'hit *that*.'

Maury was screaming at the top of the stairs. A black shadow had fallen on him and bright sprays of red jetted over the walls. Then with a grunt, the black shape launched itself across the room towards me, huge fangs aflame in the gloom. Anton dodged sideways and me, the armchair and a filing cabinet went down in an explosion of splinters, plasterwork and bricks, through the wall and into the house next door...

* * *

The next few minutes were full of fire and teeth, the sound of ripping and tearing, flesh pounding on flesh and flashes of bright, white light. I'll admit I lost my temper during that moment, and it wasn't until I slammed up against another solid wall that the red haze left my field of vision, and I could make sense of what was happening:

The room I was in was a mess. Rubble obscured everything, but I could make out a cheap broken wardrobe, a small dresser topped by a—now smashed—mirror and two mostly naked people cowering together on the remains of what was once a bed. The clanging and lights of a tram passed by in the street outside. Vinegar Tom circled dangerously like a kind of land-based shark, stopping suddenly to extend a mangled front leg: with a series of sickening cracks and pops, it stretched out into usefulness once more. It barked towards the cowering couple and a gout of flame added to their misery. I spat out a tooth.

When the Hellhound launched itself at the terrified lovers, I grabbed it by the tail and drove the spike Anton had given me into its head with a meaty crunch. There was a horrible howl, an explosion of smoke and flame—then it was gone.

'Bad dog,' I breathed and slumped to my knees.

'Um, Patrick?' Anton's voice sounded from a long way away. 'Some assistance if you could, please?'

I struggled to my feet, spike in hand and dusted uselessly at what was left of my bloodstained clothes. The terrified couple stared up at me from the ruins of their tryst, clinging together in their fear.

'No rest for the wicked,' I shrugged and made my way back to where I'd come from.

To my surprise, I found I had to make my way back through three intervening walls, passing through two other residences before I was back in Nancy Coombes' office. Fearful eyes at thrown-open doors eyed me as I jogged back, muttering "sorry!" as I went.

Anton was throwing open filing cabinets, his hat and cane lying on the desktop, when I returned.

'What's up?' I said, my mouth full of brick dust.

'Her grimoire,' he muttered, 'it's not here. She must have hidden it elsewhere.'

'Where'd she go?' I asked, examining a savage bite on my arm.

Anton jerked his chin towards the back of the house and snatched up his cane. 'She probably intends to leave by the same way I entered.'

We ran out of the office, stepping around Maury's mangled body, and headed to the open window at the end of the corridor. Anton grabbed my arm and stopped us short. An open doorway just before the window revealed a room illuminated by the dim light of a torch. It swung blindingly towards us and I threw up my hand to shield my eyes.

'Damn you!' It was Nancy's voice. 'You've ruined *everything!*'

'Take it easy lady,' I growled, 'I just saved your life.'

There was a thump and the torch moved downwards to roll on the top of a small dresser. Nancy appeared to be struggling with a drawer that finally gave way in a rush and fell to the floor. Stooping down, she picked up a heavy-looking book and stood back up, clutching it to her chest. However, I took in these details only in a secondary way; my attention was drawn to other—singular—aspects of the room:

Along each side of the chamber, were rows of hooks, about twenty in all, each one anchored a foot down from the ceiling. On these hooks were steel rings attached to leather collars, and these collars encircled the necks of naked women, hanging like coats in a cloakroom against the wallpaper. Their toes swayed two-dozen inches or so from the floorboards.

'By the Powers!' breathed Anton beside me. I gulped; I didn't know where to look.

'You may have saved my life,' said Nancy, a gleam of malice in her eye, 'but I don't intend for you to take my freedom. Shall we, ladies?'

Incredibly, horribly; *inconceivably,* the hanged women all jerked their limbs, heels drumming against the walls. Hands reached upwards to grasp the hooks and arms pulled, lifting the collars free of their restraints. All their dull, white eyes stared fixedly at Anton and me. One by one, with soft thumps, they dropped to the rug then stood upright, turning towards us.

'As I said,' Nancy purred, 'our girls aren't snowdroppers or boozehounds, and they take orders *exceedingly* well. Kill them both!'

The room filled with snarls as the score of dead women threw themselves at us. I jumped in front of Anton and began swinging my fists, one of them still handily weighted by the metal spike Anton had given me. They swarmed like rats, grabbing hold of me wherever they could lay their hands and dragging me down with their sheer, fleshy weight.

I started punching anything that looked like a face. Unfortunately, among all the physogs were distracting other things that had Brother Joseph's spittle-flecked diatribes against Sin running through my head. The grabbing and punching were bad enough, but then they began to bite.

'You should be thankful,' I heard Nancy's voice passing by to one side, 'we rarely let a client enjoy all our girls at once. And for free!' She left cackling.

I snarled and heaved, throwing most of the dead women off me, staggering to my feet, I saw Anton nearby, his sword-cane unsheathed: with a few deft swings he sliced red wounds and the women drew back in a sort of instinctive fear. It was only momentary though and they threw themselves at us once more. I grabbed one of them who had glommed me around the neck from behind and sunk her teeth into my shoulder: I punched her in the face until she fell off. It didn't stop another one taking her place.

'Have fun!' called Nancy from the head of the stairs. The dead women swarmed...

Suddenly, Nancy screamed. As she had begun to step over the corpse of her dead brother, his hand shot up and grabbed her by the leg. The scream stopped short and was replaced by lunatic laughter. Around us, all the dead women fell, inert, to the floor.

'Oh Nancy, *Nancy*,' someone said, using her voice, 'did you think I would be *so easy* to kill?' She kicked free of the corpse's hand and brushed down her skirts, still holding the old book close. 'Well, it's not what I *intended*, but it will have to do for now. And there's still a few hours until sun-up.' She smiled her cold-as-glass smile at us and threw a little wave in our direction. Rain shadows rippled across the walls.

Two shots suddenly rang out. The first punched a ragged hole in the cover of the book that Nancy clutched to her chest, spitting little pieces of flaming paper into the air. The other made a big hole in Nancy's forehead, and blood splattered the ceiling. Her hand hesitated then dropped to her side; the book hit the carpet and she toppled down the stairwell like a hundredweight of the proverbial. There was a moment of silence.

'Patrick? Are you alright?'

'*Bea!* Thank God!' I struggled to my feet and ran to the top of the stairs. At the bottom Bea stood over Nancy's ruined corpse looking up at me, holding Danny's gun—which I'd tossed away earlier—in both of her hands.

'That's Sister Immaculata, to you,' she said.

* * *

Sometime later, Anton and I sat waiting outside Father Thomas's office, decently cleaned up and clothed once more. The morning was sunny and cool and light flowed in though the clear, clean windows of the seminary. I had a black eye; a broken nose and half my head was bandaged; every time I moved—those parts I *could* move—I ached. I was feeling pain in parts of me I never even knew existed. In my lap was a small ebony box, lined in velvet and with an enamelled medallion of the Papal Seal affixed to its lid. Inside it was the rusty piece of metal that Anton had given me.

'So, a nail from the True Cross, huh?' I said.

Anton slid a sideways glance at me: he'd fared much better than me in the damage stakes, but he still had some wicked scratches across his face.

'I thought it might be of use,' he said simply, shrugging.

I grunted. 'What I want to know,' I said, 'is what is it doing *here*?'

Anton smiled, 'You think it should be chained up some-where in a Spanish cathedral? Or buried in some crypt in a Pol-ish cemetery?'

'That sounds about right' I said.

'So, who do you think would go looking for it in the sun-drenched suburb of Harris Park in Sydney, Australia?'

'I take your point,' I nodded. We both stood momentarily—me grunting and groaning—as a gaggle of nuns strode past. Once we were seated again, I raised another point:

'And this is what stopped me from being possessed by Maury Coombes?' I asked, 'except, I wasn't holding on to it at that point.'

Anton laughed. 'Correct,' he said, 'that had me confused as well for a bit. But then I spoke to Father Thomas on the telephone when it was all over, and he let me in on a little secret.'

He leaned in close, a twinkle in his eye.

'Apparently, Sister Immaculata was under orders to lace your tea with holy water.'

My jaw dropped. 'And here I thought it was just that nuns couldn't make a decent cuppa!'

Anton placed the end of his cane on the floor and spun its head around in his gloved hands, the talismans on his wrists jingling.

'I hope that this incident hasn't made you reconsider your role in our activities,' he said. 'I hope you know that you are a valuable asset in this line of work?' His face had taken on a sombre cast.

'You worried I'm getting cold feet, Anton?' I snorted. 'How many other private dicks can truthfully put "killer of Hellhounds" on their *résumé*? Don't you worry about me, sport!'

Beside me, Anton smiled and nodded. I went on, hefting the ebony box:

'But maybe we should hang onto this baby a little bit longer. Whaddaya reckon?'

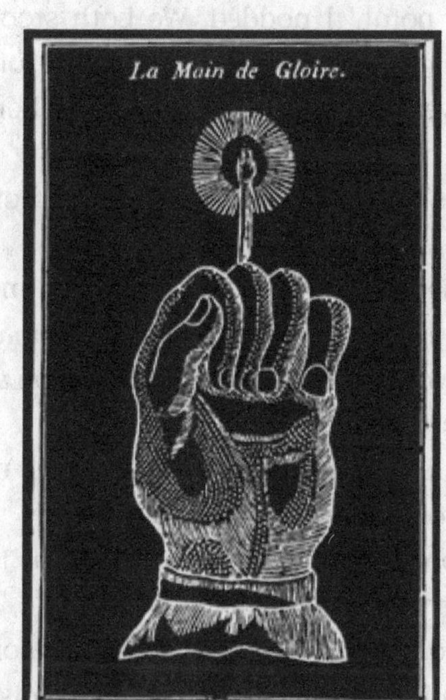

III.
"THE DEAD MAN'S KNOCK"

THE DEAD MAN'S KNOCK

---

*"NOW OPEN, LOCK! TO THE DEAD MAN'S KNOCK! FLY,
BOLT, AND BAR, AND BAND! NOR MOVE, NOR
SWERVE, JOINT, MUSCLE, OR NERVE, AT THE SPELL
OF THE DEAD MAN'S HAND! SLEEP, ALL WHO SLEEP!
—WAKE, ALL WHO WAKE! BUT BE AS THE DEAD FOR
THE DEAD MAN'S SAKE!"*

- THE INGOLDSBY LEGENDS

Fog rolled in from the darkening Pacific and rising walls of
eucalypt sparkled with the last red rays of westering sunset as the coast came into view. This was the second time in as
many days that we were headed to the southern town of Long
Bay and its gloomy gaol, the New South Wales State Penitentiary. I sat behind the wheel of the Oldsmobile, grinding my
teeth at the vehicle's ban on smoking while, beside me, Anton

pored over an old leather-bound volume, muttering occasionally and making tidy notes in a small notebook with his gold pencil.

'Looks like it could rain,' I observed, by way of clearing the tension. 'Will that affect things?'

Anton raised his head and stared out at the lightless sea for a few minutes. 'I think not,' he said at last, returning to his calculations.

I drummed my fingers on the wheel, watching the tarmac through the windscreen. Night was falling quickly along the coast and the headlights picked out the twisting white shapes of eucalypts flashing by, like ghostly sentinels of the roadway.

In short order, we came upon the town limits and I dropped the speed. Long Bay was getting ready for sleep, the lights of the few shops fading and being replaced by the sparse illumination of the houses and the tent cities. I followed the main drag past the hotel before turning onto ANZAC Parade, being careful to avoid the construction where the tramlines were being laid. Before long, the grim stone shape of the gaol loomed before us, shifting eerily in the rolling mist.

Why were we here? It seemed like only yesterday that I was striding along Campbell Street in Sydney's Haymarket, happy as Larry, listening to the Chinese jabber and watching the fireworks pop. But that was many ugly corpses and a few knuckleheaded conversations with the Law previous; a whole black tide had rolled under the bridge since then...

I shut off the engine and flicked off the lights.

'Give me a few moments to prepare myself.'

Anton seemed vague and distracted, but he was just lost in the enormity of his preparations. He stared at the imposing stone wall before us with an unfocussed brown gaze, not really seeing it so much as the litanies he was rehearsing in his head. I grunted assent and stepped out onto the road, closing the door behind me with a thunk.

It was cooler outside, the warmth of the day just starting to dissipate. I lit up a cigarette with a definite sense of relief and watched the last bloody sweeps of light fade in the west, accompanied by the raucous cries of cockatoos. While Anton got ready, I ran the last few days' events through my mind once more...

* * *

Campbell Street was ablaze with red and gold. I strode my way past a fancy, green-tiled pavilion at the top of the thoroughfare, pausing only to strike a match against one of the stone, lion-monsters standing guard there. Banners of scarlet and shop signs gold-painted in alien script drifted and swung in the light morning breeze and smells of strange cooking filled the air. I passed a window hung with ducks, flat-pressed and basted scarlet by some cooking process I couldn't identify. I dodged red lanterns and ducked small groups of children running by with strings of crackers exploding on the ends of bamboo canes. Around me, people were getting into the swing of the working day, walking with purpose, greeting each other in passing, hawking wares from kerbside trolleys: I couldn't understand a single word of it, but every bit of it made sense.

Strangely, the pieces that were most familiar were the ones that seemed out of place. A police constable walking his beat; two lads pulling bound-up stacks of the *Sydney Morning Herald* off the back of a delivery truck; a horse-drawn night-soil cart clip-clopping down a side lane, its driver belting-out *"I'm Looking Over a Four-Leaf Clover"*. Here and there, huddled clusters of young boys, pinch-faced and smoking, reminded me that I was still in the territory of the Surry Hills push, and that I'd better keep an eye on my wallet.

I stopped to get my bearings, which was probably a mistake, since a toothless old woman in black trousers immediately started badgering me to buy a cabbage from her trolley. I took the opportunity to scan my surroundings and caught sight of Anton and Ji Daoyi—along with a handful of the jacks—standing outside a doorway on a nearby side street. Breaking free of my determined vendor, I trotted over to them.

The conversation was taking place outside a laundry named the *Golden Mountain.* Several coppers were maintaining a cordon and one stood with his hands behind his back at the front door; one of them tried to prevent my approach but I stared him down and he thought better of it. There were several Chinese, looking dazed and bewildered, and Daoyi was quietly questioning them. Anton was fervently talking to the detective in charge who was playing the tough guy by the look of things. I wandered into his field of vision.

'Well, if it isn't "Kangaroo" Jack Campbell,' I said, flashing my pearly whites, 'what brings you to Chinatown so early on a workday? Getting a jump-start on your weekend laundry?'

'Dolan,' said Campbell, wincing. 'Here's trouble.'

'Not me,' I countered, 'I'm the spirit of pacifism; the very definition of *Entente Cordiale...*'

'Yeah? And what am I supposed to be? Germany?'

'I was thinking you might play England to my France,' I smiled, 'but if you'd prefer...?'

Anton rolled his eyes.

'Detective Campbell,' he said, 'please, can we adhere to the point? Ji Daoyi tells me that there has been a terrible crime committed here, concerning which he and I can lend consider-able assistance, not least because we both speak Mandarin...'

Campbell raised his hands. 'That's all well and good,' he said, 'but this is more than just a fistfight in a soap factory. And you'll probably fare no better questioning the suspects than one of my men. They're Chinese; they're like limpets. When they clam up, they stay clammed.'

'So, it's like a seaside barbecue,' I bumped a cigarette out of its packet and squinted at the gold letters across the laundry's façade.

Campbell made an exasperated noise and raised his hands again. 'Look,' he said pointedly to Anton, 'if you want to act as an interpreter, I'll need to square it with headquarters. They'll want to know how much you charge...'

'We work *pro bono*,' interjected Anton.

'...and there'll have to be a briefing on what you can and can't reveal to the public...'

'We intend to be the spirit of discretion.'

Campbell stopped and glared at Anton. At that point a Chinese woman blundered onto the scene and immediately burst into a screaming paroxysm of distress, at which several of the other Chinese hanging around rushed to her aid.

'Right Vadász,' said Campbell, 'you'll talk to witnesses and learn what they know. I'll bring you any documents to trans-late and you'll make yourself available for questions. But you don't go *anywhere* without one of my men in tow. Under-stood?'

'Perfectly,' smiled Anton

'And how's *your* Chinese, Dolan?' Campbell glared at me. 'Up to snuff?'

'I get it from my mother's side.' I blew smoke over my shoulder. He snorted and turned away to make arrangements for us with his men.

'That could've gone... more smoothly,' said Anton turning to me.

I shrugged. 'We go back,' I said, 'he's all bluff. Hello Daoyi, what's up?'

The Chinese fellow smiled at me and bowed quickly. He was about the same height as Anton, but more stoutly built and dressed in a tailored black suit with a nice charcoal stripe. He wore his hair short with a tidy moustache and he affected spats.

'I'm very well, Mr Dolan,' he said, 'as you observe. I am hoping with you it is likewise?'

'I've had a nice breakfast and a quiet stroll; I expect however, that what's happening here will be less pleasant.'

'Oh, this is quite nasty,' he said, nodding sagely, 'in fact, one might question the wisdom of having broken your fast under the circumstances.'

'That bad, huh? Don't worry—I've got a gut made of iron. What's the story?'

Anton cut in. 'This might *appear* to be merely a steam laundry,' he said waving his cane to take in the front of the building, 'but after hours, it operates as something quite different. Below-stairs is an opium den, known as the *House of the Jade Lotus*. There was some unpleasantness there last night which was announced by the day manager who came to relieve the night staff. He contacted Daoyi, who thought it wise to involve us.'

I touched the brim of my hat to Daoyi. 'Can you define the "unpleasantness"?' I asked.

'In short,' Daoyi intoned sepulchrally, 'it is murder that has been done.'

* * *

Upstairs, the *Golden Mountain* was exactly as stated: lines of washing cutting off vision; coppers topped by wringers waiting to be fired up and set to boil; the smell of damp concrete and strong soap. Behind the floor manager's desk however, there was a curtain that hid a door and a set of winding stairs heading down to the basement. From the earthy scent of it, we were moving through the foundations of the building to a short, stone-floored passage.

Our exploration stopped at a barred gate beyond which everything was hidden by a complex-patterned curtain. In front of this was a well-used chair with an old cricket bat lying on its seat. The jack who was leading us stepped forward and swung the gate wide.

'There's usually a guard posted here,' he said. 'If you ain't expected, or if you ain't paid up front, you don't get any further in.'

Anton led the way, followed by Daoyi and me. We continued through the curtain leaving our guide to deal with the gate.

I don't know what I expected an opium den to look like—not being one who frequents such places—but this seemed quite elaborate. We stepped out onto something like a wide stage with a handrail running around three sides. There was a table to the right with four chairs and a scattering of *mah jongg* tiles, while to our left was a tall sloping desk, with an open ledger lying on it and ink at the ready. A tall chair, like a fancy barstool stood behind this and, in the corner beyond, was a small couch, or daybed, covered with pillows and blankets. A brass Singapore steamer gleamed in the shadows nearby. The floorboards were covered in layers of rugs that muffled our footfalls.

Scattered around the table to the right, lay four bodies in Chinese clothes; each corpse had a bloodied face.

From this station, we could see ahead into a muted reddish gloom beyond. At the far end of the platform, stairs led down to a flagged floor, divided into four rows by a series of wooden pillars. These rows comprised banks of rude cots, screened from each other by low bamboo-weave barriers. Each cot in its small space was illuminated by a gold-tasselled red paper lantern hanging from the low ceiling, some of which had seen better days. In this area, members of the constabulary were moving to and fro and there was the occasional flash and bang of a photograph being taken. We were momentarily prevented from proceeding by two jacks frog-marching another white-faced member of their species out into the upper air: one of them carried a tin bucket which, as they passed, filled our surroundings with the smell of chunder. I noticed for the first time that several of the cots were still occupied and the shapes of those lying there were obscured by slowly-sanguinating white sheets.

Anton walked briskly down three wooden steps to the floor of the den. At the first occupied cot, he stopped and drew back the sheet that obscured the victim.

'*Isten a mennyekben...*' I knew then that things were bad. Anything that caused Anton to fall back on his native language didn't bode well.

'What've we got?' I asked.

Anton wiped his gloved hands together fussily and stood up, letting the sheet fall back in place.

'I'm not sure,' he said, 'whoever did this was very... deliberate. They seem to have taken a degree of pleasure from it. It's like... a cat? Yes?'

I knew what he was talking about. As a boy, I went rabbiting with my father. We'd run a trap line a couple of miles along a fence in the evening and then check them the next morning. If a feral cat found the line, they would eat the first rabbit they found caught in a trap and then they'd move along the line, eating less and less bunny, but still killing and dismembering anything they encountered just for the Hell of it. Usually, in one of the last traps, we'd find the cat snared, snarling and spitting, and we'd put it out of our collective misery.

'You think someone's having fun?' I asked.

Anton nodded absently, his mind whirling with details. His gaze swept the room as he replied: 'There's no indication that this man tried to defend himself, or ward off his attacker. I believe he was asleep during the process...'

I grunted. 'Well, I guess a headful of opium would help...'

Daoyi chimed in. 'If he was "chasing the dragon" perhaps,' he said, 'but I am seeing three pellets of opium here, untouched. And the pipe is clean—unused.'

The jack who'd escorted us down here materialised beside me.

'You ain't seen the best bit yet,' he grinned, 'foller me.'

He led us along the aisle to the far end of the den. There was a second raised platform here, like the one we entered by way of; unlike that set-up though, there was a row of six red doors with Chinese characters in gold painted on them. Three wooden steps led up to a walkway that ran the length of the platform in front of these doors.

'These are private rooms for the gentry,' said the constable, 'or them as don't want their pockets picked while they're dozing. You want the room second from the right.' He pointed, dropping his anchor at the top of the stairs and letting us continue, unaccompanied.

There was a bright flash and a loud bang as we approached: a police photographer stepped backwards through the door we were headed to, carrying his tripod and juggling the flash and camera. He began packing up his equipment, oblivious of our presence, whistling tunelessly under his breath. Daoyi murmured something to Anton in his native *patois* and the latter responded in kind. They were both looking at the floor, about us and back the way we had come, disapproving looks on their faces.

'What's up?' I asked lighting up a cigarette. Anton just made a rueful face and turned to the photographer.

'How many people have come in and out of this chamber since the crime was first reported?' he asked.

The shutterbug stopped what he was doing and squinted up at us. 'Dunno,' he said. 'There's me; Detective Campbell and his offsider; the doc they called in from St. Vincent's; a handful of others. Why?'

'Because there's hundreds of bloody footprints on the landing as a result, and it's now impossible to tell if any of them were left by our killer.'

The photographer looked around himself where he was crouched and noticed, probably for the first time, the large bloodstain on the threshold of the room and the myriad scarlet tracks that led in and out. He shrugged.

'If it was important, they probably would have mentioned it,' he declared.

Anton gave him a pained expression by way of answer.

'Anyway, I'm finished,' said the photographer standing and hauling his gear up over his shoulder. 'It's all yours. Hope you've got a strong stomach.' He clattered off.

It was the gateway to Hell. Inside, the room was hung with Chinese brocade and ruddily lit by sputtering scarlet lanterns, reaching the end of their oil supplies. A pair of intricately carved couches stood across from each other on either side of the room, facing the door; between them, against the far wall, was a low wooden dresser with a tray containing the numerous complex devices which I was coming to recognise as the *accoutrements* for opium smoking. A long low table occupied the floor-space between the two couches, but it had been pushed over on its side, scattering the bowls of rice and teapots that had stood on its surface. In any other circumstance, the room would have been cosy and intimate; circumstances hadn't allowed that, however.

There were two people in the chamber. On the left, lying on the couch, was a Chinese woman, naked but for a highly patterned red silk robe. She looked like she was sleeping peacefully except for the long spike protruding through the flesh of her left breast.

'Sheesh!' I said, 'can't someone cover her up? Give her a little dignity?'

'I fear she is beyond such concerns,' said Anton, 'but no doubt she would have appreciated your gallantry.'

The occupant of the other couch was in much worse shape. Like the woman, he wore only a patterned robe, this one bright yellow, patterned with flowers of some kind. In his case, the robe had been pulled down off his upper body, stripping him to the waist. Someone had rolled him over on his front, but not before slicing his belly open and dragging his guts out onto the floor: the pinkish-grey pile mingled unfortunately with the spilled rice and hovering flies. As a final insult, they'd cut his head off and replaced it, backwards, on top of his neck, stabbing his eyes out along the way.

'I guess someone really had a beef with this fellow,' I muttered.

'That would seem apparent,' replied Anton, bending quickly to look at the dead man's hands.

I turned my attention to Daoyi, who had crouched awkwardly near the girl's side. With delicate, long-nailed hands he plucked gently at her robe, re-arranging it so that she was, more or less, decently covered. Then he tapped thoughtfully at the spike that was lodged in her bosom. It was black, maybe sixteen inches long and finely tapered, with an ornately carved handled topped by a glowing white stone.

'What's that, Daoyi?' I asked.

'I believe it is what we would call a *t'an pong*,' he said; 'in English it means "spreading out rod". It is used in a gambling game. *Fan tan.*'

'That's a bad business,' I said hauling out my cigarettes, 'aren't those games all run by the Tongs?'

'Mostly,' said Daoyi, 'but this accords with who our victim over there is.' He waved a hand at the dead man.

'You know this mug?' I asked.

Daoyi nodded. 'Indeed,' he replied, 'he is *"Fan Tan"* Henry. Or Shi Chao-kong, to name him in Chinese.'

'I've heard of him,' I said; 'not a nice customer. You know who *she* is?'

Daoyi just shook his head.

'Poor thing,' I said, feeling a huge sense of injustice rise within me, 'she's just a kid. Too young to be mixed up with this kind of business!'

Daoyi glanced up at me quickly, then looked back at the dead girl's face. 'Yes, she is young,' he said quietly, 'but she knew with what she was involved. See her face? These yellow-and-grey shadows? Only one who has chased the dragon for some years wears these signs.' He stood up.

I grunted and lit my smoke.

'What have you found, Anton?' Daoyi asked.

Anton had stepped gingerly over the pile of innards on the floor and stood looking first down at the small cabinet against the wall opposite the door, then up at the low ceiling. With one grey-gloved finger, he traced a circle on the wooden surface next to the brass tray with the pipes and oil lamps.

'Hmm?' He looked over at Daoyi. 'Oh,' he pulled himself out of his thoughts. 'Questions, Daoyi,' he said, 'only questions and very little in the way of answers...'

'I need you fellows out here at the manager's post.' It was "Kangaroo" Jack appearing suddenly at the entrance to the room. 'There's a kind of register over there that may help us identify these victims.'

I snorted. 'I'd've thought you'd need no introduction to "*Fan Tan*" Henry.'

'That's him?' said Campbell. 'Well, whaddaya know. Always knew his chickens'd come home to roost one of these days.'

Anton stepped towards the doorway, careful on his feet. 'As you say, detective,' he said marshalling his hat and cane, 'we should examine this register—other patrons are, doubtless, not so infamous.'

Campbell headed off and we gingerly eased our way out of the small room. I stepped into a corner and Daoyi ducked his head and slipped out to the walkway outside. I turned and planted a foot through the doorway, trying to avoid as much of the blood as possible. Clinging to the doorframe, I shifted my weight and prepared to haul my other leg out when Anton called out to me to stop. I froze.

'Something seems to have attached itself to your shoe,' he said.

I imagined spiders; I thought of snakes; possibly scorpions.

'Well, get it off, Anton!' I hissed. 'What the hell is it?'

He leaned quickly forward and I felt him grab my ankle momentarily. When he stood up once more, he held a small square of paper in his handkerchief-shielded fingers. It was red, but whether naturally, or due to the amount of blood swamping the joint wasn't clear.

'Can I move now?' I asked.

'Hmm?' Anton responded. 'Oh! Of course, Patrick, please.' He took out his notebook and opened it: placing the red square between two blank pages, he snapped it shut again and tucked it into his jacket pocket.

'We should catch up,' he said nodding towards the others.

We re-grouped at the other end of the opium den, near the tall desk on which lay the ledger. Anton ran a finger down the list of entries on the open page and Daoyi craned his head over Anton's shoulder to lend murmured assistance. It was all Greek to me, so I walked over to the daybed and poked idly through the noisome bed linen and cushions there. Several men, in white uniforms emblazoned with the device of St. Vincent's Hospital, entered upon the scene and Campbell set them to work stretchering the victims out of the place. Under a threadbare pillow, I found a small china bowl full of rice and vegetables and a pair of chopsticks. On the floor under the bed, was a pair of dainty silk slippers.

I turned my attention to the Singapore steamer. These brass-and-glass lunchboxes are ubiquitous throughout Chinatown: essentially, they are a means of transporting hot meals from kitchens at one end of the town to hungry patrons on the other. They comprise several interconnected brass boxes held together by a frame in a cylindrical stack. A small fuel stove in the base transfers heat throughout the device keeping the food inside warm. This one was still radiating a mild cosiness.

I moseyed back over to the desk where Anton and Daoyi stood, running my eyes over the thing. Below its sloping top, was a door with an intricate padlock swinging open from an iron hasp: the door was slightly ajar.

'You said the day manager called the jacks as soon as he came in and discovered the mess?' I asked.

'This is what Detective Campbell tells me,' nodded Daoyi.

'*Sure*, he did,' I scoffed, 'first thing *after* he cleared out as much of the opium as he could.' I gently elbowed Anton aside and swung wide the door in the bottom of the desk. Inside were many small compartments, all stained by opium resin, and all empty.

'We should definitely ask him about this,' declared Anton.

'...Or whoever the woman was who was hiding in that bed over there,' I interrupted, jerking a thumb in that direction, 'presumably, the night manageress.'

'A possible witness?' Anton's eyes lit up. 'Excellent!'

He hurried across to where "Kangaroo" Jack stood overseeing things and began to impress upon him the possibility of a spectator to all these goings-on. I knocked my last Red Capstan from its packet and lit it up. On the other side of the platform, the hospital orderlies were picking up the dead Chinese and laying them in a neat row, arms crossed over their chests, prior to ferrying them out. Each of them had been stabbed brutally in the eyes. I shook my head.

'That's it,' I said to no-one in particular and moving to the exit, 'that's enough for one day...'

* * *

Ji Daoyi's digs were a short walk from the *Golden Mountain Laundry* and we all washed up there sometime later. The front of the building was advertised as the *Ruby Lantern Fortune House* and was replete with strange herbs hanging in bunches from the rafters and bottles of ill-defined things on racks about the room. Charts on the walls showed simply drawn human figures meticulously labelled in a storm of chicken-scrawl Chinese, and glass cases displayed odd assortments of dried animal and vegetable offcuts, along with rocks and intricately enamelled talismans. In the back of the building were Daoyi's consulting rooms, his office and his home, where his wife and many children went about their daily routine. Within his home environment, Daoyi had sloughed off his natty suit jacket and replaced it with a light blue silk brocade coat, emblazoned all over with twisty square knots and tiny pink bats.

Business, in Daoyi's world, inevitably started with food and, soon after we arrived, we were seated around a table in his office, tucking in to a seemingly endless procession of small but highly toothsome trifles, brought out by the eldest children in small, hot, bamboo containers. It seemed that my hunger would never be sated, but eventually, after I'd eaten an inelegant sufficiency, I was suddenly full and couldn't face another water chestnut or lotus root. I sat back groaning and happily rubbing my stomach.

'Daoyi,' I said, 'I don't know what half of that was and I can only guess what the rest might have been, but it was all bloody splendid!'

He beamed at me and nodded his head. 'Thank-you, Mr Dolan,' he said, 'you do me much honour.'

Anton had stopped eating long before me and was engrossed on the other side of the table, teaching two of Daoyi's children their letters. He carefully drew pictures on the pages of his notebook and asked them what he had depicted; when they guessed correctly, he wrote the Chinese word for it under the image and then let them try to replicate it using his propelling pencil. Finally, he gave them the word in English and checked their pronunciation.

'"Cat",' he said, carefully enunciating, '"Cat". Now you try...'

'Perhaps, at this juncture, we might discuss our findings from this morning,' said Daoyi. 'Run along, children.' He shooed them away which they did with evident reluctance.

When order had been restored, bowls cleared away and refreshing green tea provided, we settled in for a heavy talk.

'Have you had any thoughts, Anton?' asked Daoyi.

Anton put down the picture of the cat which he had drawn and smoothed it reflectively with his fingers.

'There are things about this incident which concern me greatly,' he said, speaking slowly as if marshalling his thoughts, 'but they are hidden behind outrages of unspeakable abhorrence, which serve to obscure their real import. There are veils here; layers of meaning that seek to hide method and purpose, deflecting intent and the mind behind them.'

'Tell us about them,' said Daoyi, 'elucidate them for us.' Here he indicated himself and me.

Anton straightened up in his chair. With one hand he aligned his notebook and pencil just so in front of him. The sketch of the cat smiled its inscrutable stare up at him from the tabletop.

'Let's begin with what we first happened upon,' he said. 'Patrick: what did you notice first?'

'Here we go,' I groaned, 'this is where *I* tell you what I've seen, and *you* tell me exactly what I missed and how I've been suckered into leaping to the wrong conclusions. Isn't there some other game we can play?'

Anton smiled at me and tapped a fingertip on the table-cloth. 'Unfortunately, this is the only "game" we have and—despite what you might think—your observations are at least as important to us as our own, if not moreso.' Here, he gestured to both Daoyi and himself.

'After all, Mr Dolan,' said Daoyi, 'it was *you* who discovered the fact that we may have an eyewitness to these crimes.'

I slumped back in my chair making it creak alarmingly. 'Alright,' I said, 'no need to butter me up too much.' I scratched the stubble on my chin and started recalling things.

'First, there was the *mah jongg* table on the right with all the dead guards...' I began.

'What makes you think they were guards?' broke in Anton.

"Just makes sense,' I answered, 'you need some muscle to keep order in your illegal operation; to keep out troublemakers and to stop the punters acting up. At some point, things are going to quieten down and so, you need something to keep your employees occupied. I presume that they play a fair bit of *mah jongg* and eat quite a bit in the wee hours of the morning while on shift. There was a lot of tucker in that steamer.'

'And yet,' said Anton, 'all of that "muscle" proved useless in this case.'

I shrugged. 'They must have been overwhelmed—' I started. Anton cut me off.

'—By a superior force? Four men, eliminated by a surprise assault? An attack which fails to break a single chair, or knock the bowls, or even a single *mah jongg* tile from the tabletop?'

I considered this. 'Right, I guess...'

'Now, tell me about those four dead men,' Anton continued.

Daoyi came to my aid: 'They appeared to all have been deprived of their eyes,' he said, 'a terrible way to die.'

'Indeed.' Anton turned to me again: 'Patrick, if a man armed with a knife leapt at you with the intention of stabbing out your eyes, what would you do?'

'I wouldn't let him,' I scoffed, 'and I'd hand him back his arse in an Easter basket.'

'Indeed,' said Anton, 'and yet, here we have four men, trained to fight most likely and no doubt employed for their skills in this regard, who allowed themselves to be killed in exactly this fashion, without raising a hand to defend themselves. Peculiar, no?'

We mulled this over for a bit, then Daoyi piped up.

'Poison,' he said, 'something added to the food in the steamer...' Anton was shaking his head.

'Such a tactic would have also eliminated our putative night-manageress witness, would it not? And yet, Patrick found no sign of her, apart from her shoes, despite discovering evidence that she had also partaken of the food provided. And, if our perpetrator was going to *poison* the staff at the opium den, why then take the trouble to stab out the guards' eyes afterwards?'

'All excellent points,' acknowledged Daoyi sitting back in his chair and bouncing his steepled fingertips together.

'Other things to consider,' Anton continued, 'none of the bodies in the *House of the Jade Lotus* showed signs of having tried to fight off their assailant. There was no bruising or superficial wounding, no scratches and no signs of blood, or skin, beneath their fingernails. All they bore were the clear and decisive marks of death upon their bodies. It's as if they all went to their destruction compliant and willing.'

Daoyi shuddered.

'Wait a minute,' I objected, 'you're saying that every person in that joint just lay down and *let* themselves be murdered in their sleep? Without fighting back—*at all*?'

'That's exactly what I'm saying.' Anton placed both his hands face down either side of his cat picture.

'No,' I said waving a dismissive hand, "can't be. It *must've* been the opium: they were all drugged out of their heads and didn't see it coming...'

'And that's how the authorities will no doubt choose to read the signs,' Anton replied, 'but I think not all of the victims were asleep, or drugged, when they were killed. Some of them were very much awake and aware of what was happening to them.'

'Horrible,' Daoyi shuddered.

'I'm sorry,' I countered, holding up my hands in disbelief, 'I just can't see it...'

'Have you heard of Optography?' Anton cut me off with a *non-sequitur.*

'Nope,' I said, 'I don't need spectacles...'

'Not Optometry,' he said, '*Optography*. A different thing altogether.'

'I, too, am in ignorance about this, Anton,' said Daoyi sitting forward once more, 'please to enlighten.'

Anton relaxed back in his chair. 'Optography is a questionable science,' he said, 'a largely discredited area of research from last century that, nevertheless, still makes its presence known periodically. Essentially, it is based on the idea that whatever a creature sees just as its death occurs—particularly if it is a *violent* death—remains imprinted upon the retinas of its eyes and can, through photographic processes, be preserved and revealed to others. Although repeated experimentation has shown no viability in the idea, due to its promotion in the writings of such people as Edgar Allan Poe and Jules Verne, it remains as a kind of *idée fixe* in the popular imagination, to the extent that, every few years or so, a police investigation, or a courtroom trial, dabbles with the notion in order to bring about a verdict in an unsolved crime.'

'I heard it was a pack of cobblers,' I said, 'and that, even if it *was* true, we don't have the means of making it work properly, or of being any practical use.'

'Is it spoken of in your community, Daoyi?'

Daoyi shook his head. 'I—personally—have never heard of such a thing. I cannot speak for all of my compatriots, but it is not discussed in my culture, to my knowing at least.'

Anton was nodding. 'That's what I thought,' he declared, 'and that's why I think not all of the victims here were in the grip of opium abuse when they were killed, and also why I think the killer was not Chinese.'

'What?' I said. 'How do you come to *that* conclusion?'

'*I* believe that Optography is—as you say—"a pack of cobblers"; but I think that our murderer not only knows of it, but thinks that it might possibly have merit, and that it could be used to identify him as the culprit. That's why he destroyed the eyes of certain of his victims, which automatically implies that they were awake, if not mobile, and conscious of their own destruction.'

I stood up sharply and walked around my chair, leaning heavily on the back of it. 'Let me get this straight,' I said, 'the guards; "*Fan Tan*" Henry; they were all butchered like dogs, aware what was happening to them, and yet unable to move, or do *anything* to stop it? What about the night manageress? Who's to say she didn't poison the guards and off them herself, before pulling a midnight flit out to whoop-whoop with all that opium?'

'I think she was incapacitated also,' said Anton, 'but, being hidden within the bedclothes behind the desk, the killer missed her presence and she was thus spared.'

'So, she just lay there under the covers, unable to move, listening to everyone else in the place getting gutted like a haul of fish?'

'You have it,' said Anton, 'now...'

'*I have it, bollocks!*' I yelled. '*How* does that happen? How *can* it happen? It's crazy!'

A door to one side cracked open slightly and a soft voice murmured in Chinese. Daoyi made soothing responses and the door shut again.

'Please, Mr Dolan,' he said to me, 'sit down and have some more tea.'

I circled my chair again and sat down with a grunt, leaning forward on my elbows.

'Hell's bells, Anton,' I shuddered, 'it gives me chills even thinking about it. What makes it happen?' I asked. 'What could *do* something like that?'

By way of reply, he slid the drawing of the cat over to me, orientating it so that its slitted eyes looked up into mine. 'Something evil,' he said; 'something very old and completely without mercy.'

* * *

'That deals with one layer of our mystery,' Anton continued after a pause. 'However, there is another aspect to this puzzle which must be resolved.'

I groaned and rubbed my forehead; Daoyi sat up in his seat and leaned forward.

'As I said, there are layers of obfuscation in this crime, not all of which are intentional, but which serve, regardless, to obscure the nature of the attack and its author. The killing of the staff and patrons of the *Jade Lotus House* forces us to think that the attack was indiscriminate, that it was untargeted; but upon closer inspection this proves not to be the case. Those deaths, the cruelty and dispassion of the violence, reveal the tenor of the mind at work here; but his *motivation*, this is outlined by another set of evidence.'

Anton picked up his notebook and flipped to the back, prising apart two dark-stained pages. This opening he displayed to Daoyi, who craned his head forward uncertainly.

'I am fairly certain of what this is,' said Anton, 'but I would like you to confirm that for me Daoyi.'

Daoyi had reached forward a questing hand but stopped before touching the object revealed before him. 'Is that blood?' he asked.

'Unfortunately,' Anton confirmed.

Daoyi sat back in his seat, a fastidious hand hovering before his nose. 'It looks like a *kau li*,' he said, 'you would say "dog's tongue" in English. It is a betting chit used in *fan tan*.'

Anton turned the notebook to let me see: it was the square of red paper which he had twitched off my boot sole as we were leaving the bloody chamber. In the clear, honest light of Daoyi's office, I could see that two letters had been written upon it in ink, along with a series of increasing numbers, the earlier ones crossed out by blood-blurred strokes. Taken altogether I could make out "C.Q." and "-£1,200".

'Can I take it to mean that this C.Q. owes someone a Hell of a lot of money?'

Anton closed the book once more allowing Daoyi to visibly relax. 'This is my reading of it also,' he acknowledged, 'and thus, we come to the heart of our crime.'

'You're telling me that this—nightmare—was all just to wipe out—a *gambling debt*?' I was incredulous.

Anton nodded gently. 'Our criminal is of a particular frame of mind. He is intelligent, careful and measured; however, he is also human and prone to human foibles. The game of *fan tan* is peculiarly ritualised, surrounded by strange observances and complex ceremonies; our criminal is attracted to such mysticism and, in his arrogance, feels certain that he can penetrate its mysteries with ease and—what is the expression?—take the house for every last penny?' I snorted.

He continued. 'Unfortunately, *fan tan*, like every organised gambling activity, is heavily weighted in *favour* of the house, and before he knew it, he was in debt to "*Fan Tan*" Henry for a vast sum, without the means to re-pay it.'

'He thinks he's so smart and he doesn't realise that gambling is just a tax on stupidity?'

'I'm sure that's a lesson he has recently taken to heart, Patrick. Unfortunately, our killer is unable to separate the gambling process—and his lack of skill with it—from the notion that he has been deliberately targeted for humiliation. For him, this slight is a personal offense, and so he has bent his will towards revenge.'

'This is just getting worse,' I rubbed my face briskly with my hands. 'Do we know who this chucklehead is? Have your insights gotten us that far?'

Anton tapped his notebook. 'We now know his initials, a fact which is of invaluable assistance, and we know a few further things more which are revealing.'

Daoyi and I looked at each other momentarily. 'We do?' I asked.

Anton nodded and began ticking things off on his fingers.

'First,' he stated, 'he kills the girl with a *fan tan* rod. This is deliberate: a robbing of his nemesis, taking from him something precious, just as something precious of his own—his pride, probably; nothing as tawdry as money—was taken from him. At this point, the girl is dead, and he spends no more time on her: she means nothing to him, and he freely demonstrates this fact to his victim, to underscore the point. Remember that "*Fan Tan*" Henry is awake and watching all the time that this is happening.'

I winced; Anton went on.

'Next, he begins his work on his enemy. In Roman times, the Germanic tribes had a spiritual connexion to the trees which formed the physical barrier that helped repel the Roman invasions. Harming a tree could result in the perpetrator being sacrificed to atone for their sin. One way that they did this was by cutting out a sinner's navel, nailing this to the damaged tree, and forcing them to run around and around it, eventually wrapping the tree trunk in their own entrails. A life is given for a life; balance and order restored...'

'I don't follow,' I interjected. Daoyi raised a finger.

'I believe I do,' he said. 'Our criminal perceives himself to be the same as those German trees; he feels he is... how is it said in English, Mr Dolan? He is a "local column"...?'

'You mean, a "pillar of the community"? He thinks he needs to be shown respect.'

'Exactly,' Anton approved. 'Rather than wind Mr Shi's insides around a tree however, he took the rather unpleasant option of just slowly pulling them out from within, a process which, I need hardly point out, is lengthy and painful. It's why the English used to execute treasonous prisoners in just such a fashion.'

I shook my head, banishing the unpleasant imagery. 'Alright—he kills the girl; then he guts Henry, but slowly: what about the rest of it?'

'Ah! This is interesting!' Anton ticked off another finger. 'Having killed—or *almost* killed—"*Fan Tan*" Henry, our killer needs to ensure that there are no repercussions...'

'The bit with the eyes, right?' I said.

'Yes, but remember that our murderer has other, higher, ritualistic concerns driving his madness. First, he decapitates his enemy, killing him off finally if he is not already dead by now. Then he turns the body over, so that it faces downwards. Why do this? What do these things signify? I recognised them almost immediately since this is often done to the dead in my home country before they are buried.'

'Really? What for?'

'To prevent them coming back to a semblance of life and seeking revenge.'

There was a lengthy silence.

'That's insane,' I said at last.

'As is our killer,' Anton replied. 'I submit that he tortured and killed "*Fan Tan*" Henry in response to a perceived humiliation, then arranged his body to prevent him rising from the dead and seeking vengeance. Finally, he stabbed Mr Shi's eyes out to prevent the possibility of the ill-defined science of optography identifying him.'

I rubbed my face taking this all in. Daoyi broke our ruminations:

'There is only one question, which keeps coming back to my thoughts,' he said: 'How? How can it be that this person can do all of this without being interrupted or prevented?'

Anton was nodding while Daoyi brought up this pertinent point.

'It's obscure,' he said, 'but there is a way. A method which could allow a killer to do all we've discussed, and more.' He straightened his notebook and pencil again, placing them on top of his cat drawing.

'Tell me,' he said, 'Have either of you ever heard of a Hand of Glory?'

* * *

Our blank expressions must have spoken volumes.

'Its origins are shrouded,' he said; 'in French it is called "*Main de Gloire*", which some believe is a corruption of the word "mandragora", the name of a plant associated with the sites of gallows. Regardless, it is a talisman used to open locks and render the occupants of a building paralysed—deeply sleeping if they were in that state already, at the moment that the spell was invoked; aware, but unable to move, if they were awake at that time.

'According to the lore, the one who creates and wields the Hand of Glory can see in darkness and can bypass all barriers to their goal. They are free to enact any atrocity they please upon their victims, without fear of reprisal—as long as they take appropriate measures to avoid identification.'

Daoyi reached behind him to a nearby bookcase grabbing a notepad and pencil. He licked the point quickly and held it over the blank page.

'How does one make this talisman?' he asked.

Anton smiled. 'There are several recipes in the many grimoires which touch upon the topic, but there is little consensus amongst them. They all begin though, with the acquisition of the hand of a hanged man...'

'Not something that you can just pick up at the local grocers,' I scoffed.

'No, indeed,' said Anton, 'and even rarer in these days when the value of capital punishment is being debated at the highest levels.'

'Once the hand is obtained,' he continued, 'it must be pickled and smoked, and the fat squeezed out of it and collected. The recipes for these treatments are hopelessly contradictory and riddled with errors, so immediate success can hardly be assured.' Daoyi put down his pencil.

'Some grimoires call for the collected fat to be formed into a candle, with a hair of the hanged man to be used as the wick. The pickled hand, in these instances, is contrived to hold this item, and the lighting of it sets the spell in motion; other accounts require the hand to be dipped in this tallow and the extended fingers themselves are used as the candles, meaning that the talisman has a limited duration of usefulness.'

'Like, five shots and done?' I asked. Anton shrugged.

'Possibly,' he said, 'there's little that is concrete in the sources, as is typical.'

'And what are these sources,' broke in Daoyi, 'are they available such that our killer could find one?'

'There is useful information in the *Compendium Maleficarum* by Guazzo, dated 1608,' said Anton, 'but that is not an easily found work. That being said, practically every copy of the *Petit Albert* has a recipe for making a Hand of Glory and there are always a number of versions of that book circulating about...'

'What's a "Petty Owl Bear"?' I asked.

'It's a grimoire,' Anton explained, 'a book of magic spells. It is supposed to be derived from the private magical workbooks of Albertus Magnus, dating from the 1700s, but the attribution is tenuous. Whenever it is found, it is usually cheaply printed and crudely assembled. As often as not, it combines elements of other works of little, or greater, merit and two copies are rarely ever the same. Mostly, it is a means of parting the credulous from their money.'

'We have this also,' Daoyi chimed in, '*Pao Pu Tzu*, or *Tan Chin Yao Chueh*, are often claimed, but mostly they are a trick.'

'What is most concerning in this instance,' said Anton, 'is that our killer seems to have a source which details the correct method of manufacture. If we can, we should try and obtain his notes and texts, in order that this might never happen again.'

I held up a hand. 'Alright,' I said, 'let's assume that something like this Hand of Glory can be made and someone out there can make one. How do you know? I mean, it's a colourful idea, I grant you, but how do you know it's here? That this is happening? What's your proof?'

Anton sat back in his seat and gathered his thoughts. Finally, he said, 'in this kind of an investigation, we must examine every clue presented to us, no matter how small. Every piece of evidence is vital to the understanding of the event; if something is overlooked, it could mean that the puzzle will never be solved. This explains my chagrin upon finding the floor covered with the boot marks of all Detective Campbell's men. Fortunately, there are times when pieces of the story cancel each other out, rendering certain elements redundant—that was the case in this instance. Once all the pieces have been found, it remains only to weave a narrative around them that satisfies all the elements of the story; or, if you will, one has simply to find a frame which will hold every part of the picture. In most instances, only one such frame will fit.

'Do you remember that, in Mr Shi's room, there was a cabinet against the wall opposite the door which had upon it a brass tray with all of the equipment necessary for smoking opium?'

'Sure,' I said, 'I watched you messing with it.' Daoyi nodded agreement.

'Next to that tray, on the lacquered wood of its top surface, I found a circle of greasy wax, not unlike that formed when a candle is placed directly onto a table without the benefit of a candlestick. This tallow was very oily and unlikely to completely harden, and I knew it was poorly made because its burning left dark sooty marks on the low ceiling, just above.

Before I found this clue, I had only a vague notion of the possibility of a Hand of Glory being used; with these signs I now had a frame that would contain everything that we had discovered.' He stopped and looked at both of us, one after the other.

'Right,' I said, 'you've sold me...'

At this point, there was a knock at the door and one of Daoyi's older children stuck his head into the room. He murmured something to his father, and they had a brief exchange: Daoyi expressed sudden excitement and stood up.

'Gentlemen!' he exclaimed, 'Good news! It seems that the night manageress has been found and wishes to speak with me. We should go at once!'

I stood up, but Anton held up a hand: 'You two both go,' he said, 'I need to do some research. Can we meet up at my abode this evening?'

Daoyi nodded once sharply and turned to leave, talking ten to the dozen with his son. I looked at Anton.

'What's on your mind?' I asked.

He stood up and retrieved his notebook and pencil from the tabletop. 'I need to find out when the most recent hanging took place, and where. I think some of my friends at the offices of *The Sun* will be able to assist me.'

As we made to leave, I saw the picture of the cat on its scrap of notepaper, lying discarded on the tabletop. Reaching out I picked it up, folded it and tucked it into my fob pocket. Anton raised a quizzical eyebrow at me.

'Just a little something to keep me focussed on what we're looking for,' I said. 'C'mon—let's get out of here: I'm dying for a smoke.'

* * *

I'm not sure what you'd call Ji Daoyi. He sells odd mixtures and potions from his shop on the high street and performs some kind of medicine and massage on the wounded, along with a weird routine that he does with long needles—I've had first-hand experience on how effective he is with this stuff, since he's operated on me a couple of times since I started working with Anton. But that's just part of it: people come to him for advice, on everything from how to plan a building, to running a business, to starting a family—his word is the good oil amongst the Chinese and they treat him like a village elder. That being said, it was really only a matter of time before word would reach him concerning the whereabouts of the night manageress.

After leaving Daoyi's place, we crossed Campbell Street and wandered into the back-alleys on the far side. As we walked, people stopped what they were doing and pointed at us: some of them started to follow along, talking to Daoyi who nodded sagely every so often, and pointing ahead excitedly. We came to a crossroads and headed to a small business, the door of which opened onto the corner junction of two of the lanes. Standing in this doorway was a well-muscled older fellow in black pyjamas, who looked somewhat disconcerted by the sudden appearance of all these people. Daoyi stopped before him and bowed low. After a short conversation, during which the front door man kept shooting worried glances at yours truly, he agreed to let us in.

I stooped down next to Daoyi, ostensibly to grind out my cigarette, but really in order to murmur in his ear: 'What is this joint, Daoyi?'

'This place is called *Resplendent Phoenix*,' he replied *sotto voce*, 'it was "*Fan Tan*" Henry's gambling parlour.'

'Figures,' I muttered.

'We are fortunate,' he went on, 'that the previous owner is suddenly dead in strange circumstances—a new leader has not yet risen to replace him, and these people are seeking guidance.'

'Well,' I smiled broadly, 'ain't we in l—'

'No, no, no, no, no!' Daoyi cut me off worriedly. 'We never speak of fortune when entering such a place! To do so is most... unwise.' He trailed off lamely.

'Alright,' I replied, 'consider me told.'

We went in and, to say that this was the most unusual Chinese business I'd ever been in, that would be an understatement. The place was bare. It wasn't just that there was a distinct lack of the sort of ornamentation I'd come to expect of Chinatown, it was that this place was as pared back as a Lutheran church. The floor was just bare boards and the walls were whitewashed, the paint strokes ending crudely at that point which the tallest painter could reach. From the middle of the ceiling a bare bulb hung down on a length of flex, which had also been painted white. As far as phoenixes go, the only thing "resplendent" about this one would have to be its personality. And what I'd seen of *that* so far, wasn't inspiring.

In the middle of the floor, tacked down with small nails, was a square made up of four strips of copper, or brass, gleaming from having been polished by the passing of many feet. The strips were about two inches wide and the whole square about three feet across. Liberal use of the whitewash meant that each side of the square was highlighted by a Chinese letter. Across the expanse of floorboards, hundreds of those red, square betting-slips were scattered, mounding up into drifts in the corners.

There was a wide doorway opposite the entrance on the left-hand wall through which we could see many people seated and eating, although conversation was notably lacking. Smells of Chinese cooking billowed into the room along with the sounds of a kitchen in full swing; I felt my stomach growl. Next to this door, angled into the far corner, was a long-worn table with small boxes and jars on its top; seated on a stool at this sole piece of furniture was a Chinese woman, ignoring chopsticks and a steaming bowl of rice and vegetables placed before her. She was barefoot and a grease-stained canvas bag, held closed with a leather strap, lay on the floor beneath her seat. She was staring blankly off into space.

Daoyi knelt down in front of her and took both of her hands in his, murmuring quietly. I sat down on the table edge and, because I had to move the bowl of unwanted food any-way, I picked up the chopsticks and hoed in.

These Chinese dames, it's hard to pin down how old they are. They're either younger than you think or older than you can believe, and this lady was no exception. She was shook up though and lacking that poise which seems to be the hall-mark of her sisters. She was wearing one of the close-fitting dresses the Chinese ladies like to wear out on the town, black silk patterned all over with green-leaved branches bearing tiny pink-and-scarlet flowers. Her hair was coming loose, and she'd obviously been turning on the waterworks at length. It looked as though she'd just run out of steam.

'Leiping! Leiping!' Daoyi urged softly, shaking her gently by the shoulder. There was no response. He stood and walked be-hind her, placing his hands upon her neck and applying mild pressure.

'Mr Dolan,' he said, 'Please to assist? Could you take her arms and hold them together out in front?'

'Sure,' I said, chewing. 'Say Daoyi—what's this?' I held up something with my chopsticks.

'Is bamboo shoot,' he said.

'That's like grass, right?' He nodded. I shrugged and ate it anyway.

Standing up, I grabbed both the lady's hands in my own and held her limbs out at full stretch, Daoyi indicating a higher or lower angle with a hand gesture. Her head lolled forward onto her arms. At a particular moment, Daoyi applied quick pressure to her back with his elbow.

She came back to life in a rush, babbling wildly and trying to stand up. When she clapped eyes on me, they went wide, and she began to scream and struggle. Daoyi moved hurriedly into her field of vision and took over the handholding, calming her down with soothing noises. She sat back down, only then seeming to realise where she was, and the two of them began a rapid-fire conversation. Beside us, the door to the kitchen was filled with dispassionate observers dipping into their bowls and quietly chewing. I raised the empty bowl I held and shrugged, gesturing to the hysterical woman: it couldn't hurt to try.

Pretty soon, all that was going to be said had been said, and Leiping was simply shaking and crying. Daoyi reached for his hat and helped her to her feet.

'We must return to the *Ruby Lantern*,' he said, 'she is well, but needs rest and time to overcome the shock.'

'Right.' I got to my feet, glaring at the gathered spectators for not having had the sense of charity to bring this harried woman (and her protectors) one measly bowl of food, and got under my hat. 'What about this?' I picked up the canvas bag from off the floor.

'Leave it there,' said Daoyi. 'It holds the drugs from the *Jade Lotus*. In her panic, Leiping took them and brought them here, afraid that the owners of the *Resplendent Phoenix* would enact vengeance against her employers in retaliation for "*Fan Tan*" Henry's murder. She thought it might—what is the expression?—smooth things over?'

I nodded and dropped the bag back down on the newly vacated stool. Straightening my tie, I was about to leave when something caught my eye: on the floor under the edge of the table, several oily blobs had coagulated on the dusty floorboards; above them, a pearly trail of the stuff dribbled off the edge of the tabletop, fuelled by a semi-circle of the same waxy material. I looked up quickly: the ceiling was too high to show signs of greasy smoke, but a thrill slid down the length of my spine anyway, chilling me with realisation—our killer had been here with his magic trinket.

I rushed out of there to catch up with Daoyi, trying to get as far away from the evil *juju* as possible...

* * *

By the early hours of that evening, we had gathered together once more, this time in Anton's swanky rooms in his villa overlooking Woolloomooloo. It was a memorable get-together, for me at least—of my handful of visits, it was the first time I didn't clock my head on the stuffed crocodile hanging from the ceiling.

We were led in by Tegbir, Anton's inscrutable Sikh manservant. He took our coats and hats from us in the front hall, then led us through the library—around the crocodile—and into the main parlour. As we entered, Anton came in from his office which let into the room from another side.

'Supper will soon be ready,' murmured Tegbir and evaporated.

The room was long and airy with a high ceiling. Two doors gave access—the one from the library which Daoyi and I had come in by, and the other on the adjacent wall that led to Anton's *sanctum sanctorum*. The other two walls were pierced by French windows letting out onto the porch which ran around the three sides of the building facing the street. The room was occupied by several glass cases—some holding more books; others containing odd-looking artefacts that Anton had collected—and a large terrestrial globe stood in one corner. Old paintings of South Seas scenes hung from the walls and potted palms lent a genteel aspect to the space.

Running along the centre of the room was a long table, with several padded armchairs standing against it. A neat row of old books had been arranged along its length and over one end had been draped a striking *ikat* weave cloth: on this were deployed small stacks of crockery and cutlery, the bases of several silver chafing dishes and a tall gleaming samovar. My stomach growled in approval.

'Please sit,' Anton gestured and we both hurried to comply.

A cooling breeze blew through the room gently stirring the curtains by the windows a muted hum of hoofbeats and footsteps—broken occasionally by the purr of a car engine—provided a soothing backdrop. A rumble of thunder broke through intermittently.

'I believe we might expect rain soon,' said Daoyi, running two fingers slowly along the edge of the table.

Anton pulled his watch from his pocket and glared at it. 'In a little while,' he acknowledged. He held a book in his hand and pushed it across the table towards me.

'This is Guazzo's *Compendium Maleficarum*' he said, 'the marked page shows an interesting image.'

The volume was small and square-ish, about an inch thick. The covers were of some stiff white material and highly decorated with gold lettering and scrollwork; a plain parchment bookmark highlighted a page which I flipped open to.

'Huh,' I grunted.

The plate showed a disembodied hand standing on its stump of a wrist. The fingers were curled into a loose fist, and each one was indicated with a letter from some alphabet I didn't recognise. Between the first and second digits, a large candle had been placed and a jaunty flame issued from the wick. Below the image ran the title *"La Mano della Gloria"*.

'So that's it,' I said handing the book to Daoyi.

'It's one visual treatment,' Anton replied, 'and the one which is most often borrowed for other works.' He flipped open another volume from the line on the tabletop—the lurid contents and cheap paper gave the lie to the handsome leather binding which contained it. An almost exact duplicate of the illustration from the first book presented itself.

'This is how it looks in the *Petit Albert*.'

'You said that it might not look like this exactly,' Daoyi closed his book and slid it back to the centre of the table.

'That's true,' Anton replied, 'and that is the most essential trouble with this case: the sources are a mess. Nothing grasps the essence of the tool involved; there are too many variables, alterations in recipes and recitations, terms and processes.

And yet, we know that someone out there in the world has found the true path and made it work.'

He grabbed another volume and took from beneath it a neat book of approximately the same size but more like an accountant's ledger in appearance.

'I have gathered here, all of the relevant sources for the Hand of Glory along with their transcriptions into English,' he said, 'I propose that we go through them and identify the essential factors which are agreed upon across all of them.' Beside me Daoyi nodded briskly; I doubt the expression on my face could have been interpreted as "joy" or "excitement". Fortunately, Tegbir appeared at that point, his arms laden with steaming dishes of curry.

'Supper first, of course,' sighed Anton.

Now this was something I could *really* get interested in. We launched upon a pleasant interval of savouring the fruits of Tegbir's homeland cuisine, washed down with the good hot tea with which Tegbir kept our glasses filled. Tegbir always claimed that he spiced the meals he prepared for us with a light hand, unsure that our alien palates could deal with it turned up full bore; he made sure to direct our attention to a small salver with a pot of cream and a jug of milk, which were to be our remedies if the heat became too intense. I always took the opportunity to dare him to up the ante, claiming invincibility in the gustatory department, and he always demurred saying that I had no idea what kind of trouble I would be letting myself in for. Anton, raised on his native Hungarian peppers, said that even *he* had difficulty with the full might of Tegbir's technique. With Daoyi there—no stranger to the hot stuff himself—the banter flew thick and was followed by much laughter. An agreeable time was had by all.

Finally though, the dishes were cleared away and we started to work the books. Rain had started to fall during the meal and the task we embarked upon was punctuated by the grumbling of thunder. For myself and Daoyi, this boiled down to making and checking lists of ingredients, combing through each different recipe and looking for the instances when the spells agreed upon what was supposed to be used where and when. For my part, this was so much gobbledygook. Anton contented himself with reading each method thoroughly and making notes in his neat hand.

'What the Hell is "zimat"?' I asked, throwing down my pencil.

Anton kept flipping through his book as he replied: 'I believe it refers to sesame seeds,' he said.

'"Open Sesame", huh?'

Anton smirked. 'Something along those lines perhaps...'

Daoyi closed his dictionary with a thump. 'I am wondering about a certain point,' he said, 'which is somewhat unclear in these sources: does the Hand allow access into a building, and *then* opens all other locks within that structure, or must the maker first enter the building before lighting the Hand, thereafter enjoying its benefits?'

'It's an interesting point,' Anton put down his pen, 'is the Hand limited by being within the bounds of a fixed environment? Or does its effect travel with it wherever the wielder moves?'

'There doesn't seem to be a comment about this anywhere.' Daoyi shrugged and spread his hands over the books.

'Yes, it is very frustrating.'

I fell back in my chair and tossed my pencil on the tabletop.

'How'd you get on at *The Sun*?' I asked.

Anton put the cap back on his fountain pen and laid in carefully in the gutter of the book which lay open in front of him.

'With moderate success,' he said, 'I have procured a list of all the most recent executions performed within the state across the last twelve months. It is quite revealing.'

'I'm glad something is,' I growled. 'What did you get?'

'We are limited by the spell's process,' Anton stated. 'As we've all discovered, the creation of the Hand of Glory must take place during the so-called "dog days", which, in the Northern hemisphere, occur roughly following the appearance of the star Sirius in the heavens in the middle of June. Here in the south, this must be reinterpreted correctly in order to succeed. Is the appearance of the star the crucial factor? Or are the hot and humid effects of the season the required ingredient? Again, the sources are not explicit.

'I have created a list of executions which take into account proximity to these times,' he went on, 'and it is by no means lengthy. The most likely candidate would seem to be one Eugene Lowell, executed for killing his wife and child last August.'

'Now we're getting somewhere,' I sat forward eagerly.

'...And running into further difficulties. Lowell was executed at the State Penitentiary for Men and access to him and his remains was limited to a very few individuals; finding hanged murderers is no longer a matter of simply wandering down to the village crossroads, as it was back in the 1600s.'

I scratched at my chin with a thumbnail. 'But isn't that a good thing?' I said. 'The fewer people who dealt with him and his remains, the smaller the pool of suspects, right?'

'I admit, it is a small bright spark in this lengthy dark tunnel,' Anton agreed, 'however, it implies that there might be corrupt individuals within the penal system, and this forces us to tread very carefully indeed.'

'There are "corrupt individuals" everywhere, Anton. Why should gaolers be excused?'

He shrugged, acknowledging the point. 'It simply means that we need to have a light touch and to keep our wits about us from here on in.'

'Where is this Lowell buried?' asked Daoyi. 'Is it possible that, once beneath the ground someone might have dug him up again to get what was needed? Someone who is not of the gaol?'

'It's possible,' Anton sat back stroking his beard. 'Gentlemen, I believe our next set of inquiries should take place at Long Bay. I suggest that we travel there and see what we might find.'

Daoyi pushed back his chair and stood up. 'I wish you every success,' he said bowing, 'however, I have duties which will keep me here in Town. Now, it is quite late and I must be going home. Thank you for your company, gentlemen and many thanks, Anton, for this so pleasant evening.'

We stood up and escorted Daoyi to the front door where Tegbir waited, holding his coat and hat. We watched as he trudged down the tiled path to the road and then headed up Victoria Street towards King's Cross. As he passed from view, I stretched and yawned hugely.

'I guess I'd better hit the hay, too,' I said, 'looks like tomorrow could be a big day.'

'You're welcome to the guest room...' Anton offered.

I squinted out into the drizzly evening. 'Y'know, I just might take you up on that,' I said, 'after all, it's a bit of a step to Long Bay and we'll need an early start.'

* * *

We left before dawn, running the Oldsmobile out towards Bondi and then down the coast road, through Bronte and Coogee—the sun came up as we passed through Maroubra, blazing in a blue-and-rose sky, strewn with the fleeting clouds that signalled the end of the night's rain. Some minutes later, we descended into Long Bay proper, passing a sign which welcomed us to the "Village of Brand", Long Bay's real name and one which very few people ever used.

Anton cruised down to the promenade paralleling the beach and came to a halt at a small picnic area. As soon as the engine stopped, I kicked open the door and stepped out to light a cigarette, stretching as I did so. Below us the beach curved prettily around towards the scrubby headland, edged by a series of small tent clusters, their canvas roofs shining in the morning light. Beyond lay an expanse of rugged bushland, cut through by roads and punctuated by the signs of a growing settlement. A pleasant breeze blew in across the waves.

At a signal from Anton, I went back to the car and we trundled our way towards the centre of town, me behind the wheel this time. As we neared the intersection of ANZAC Parade and Prince Edward Street, we noticed a small tea rooms open for business. A group of labourers, huddling in the morning freshness, were buying breakfast before the day got under way: what with buildings going up on all sides and tramlines being dug into the roads, "Brand" gave off the air of a burgeoning community. Anton indicated that we should stop and soon we were seated at a small table in the crowded eatery. Anton sipped his brew and winced.

'Not the best,' he said. 'I actually prefer coffee first thing in the morning.'

'Good luck with that, out here in the sticks,' I snorted.

He took out a small valise and opened it up, flicking through a sheaf of papers within, making sure that he had all that he needed.

'What's our approach?' I asked, buttering a thick slice of toast.

'Ours is a spiritual path,' he replied. 'I have a letter of introduction from Father Thomas, asking for an interview with the prison chaplain and an inspection of the facilities. He has also coached me in some questions pertaining to the prisoners' spiritual well-being.'

'Good ol' Father Thomas.' I was muffled by toast and jam.

'Yes,' Anton agreed, 'John Tomlinson is the current chaplain at the gaol, and of the Anglican faith. We felt it only natural to undertake our foray as parties observing the treatment and succour of Catholic felons.' He sipped his tea once more and made another face. '*Why* must they always put milk in, without asking?'

'Welcome to whoop-whoop!'

We finished up and returned to the Oldsmobile; in short order we were knocking at the front gate of the NSW State Penitentiary for Men. Through the gate, we could see the imposing façade—two squat towers surmounted by a triangular pediment, like a Norman fortress playing with the idea of a portico. The sleepy guard at the front gate reviewed Anton's letter and then directed us to the visitors' entrance; in short order we were seated on uncomfortable chairs in the corridor outside the Chaplain's Office.

Our surroundings were drab and bare, with flat, green-enamelled walls and linoleum tiles on the floor. Windowed wooden doors lined the hallway, each signified by a blue number on a small tin plate—the Reverend's door broke the mould by the addition of a small wooden cross tacked up to the left of the glass above the doorknob. A strong smell of cabbage permeated the place. Shortly after nine o'clock, a bustling slight figure in black with spectacles approached us, juggling an armful of ledgers.

'Let me help you with that,' I said as he drew near and took the paperwork from him. He gaped at us like a goldfish, eyes swimming behind thick lenses, only just realising we were there to see him. He hauled a key from his pocket and rattled it in the lock of his office door.

'I'm sorry,' he said at last. 'Have we met?'

Anton swooped in to shake hands. 'We have a letter of introduction,' he said; 'we'd like to make some inquiries if that's no problem.'

Disengaging, Reverend Tomlinson, stepped into the office and snapped on the lights. He turned to take back his ledgers and dumped them on the desk, then took the letter which Anton held out to him.

'This is most unfortunate,' he said smoothing his hand over his oiled blonde hair, 'I have a busy morning with Superintendent Quilter lined up...'

'Quilter, huh?' I interrupted, 'I knew some Quilters once. What's his first name?'

The Reverend blinked at me, caught off guard. 'Charles,' he said, 'but surely it must have been some other family...'

I shrugged and turned to face Anton. Out of sight of the chaplain, I mouthed "C.Q." at him and quirked my eyebrows. He rolled his eyes in response.

'I understand that you are busy and that our arrival without an appointment is inconvenient,' he said to Tomlinson, 'we are quite happy to wait for your meeting to finish...'

'That's just it,' he replied, 'I've no idea how long this will take—we're combing through the accounts for the last year looking for ways to moderate our expenditure. We could be at it all day.'

Anton winced. 'Then perhaps we could make an appointment to meet at some later time. Until then, would it be possible to have a tour of the facilities? Perhaps with one of your subordinates?'

'"Subordinates"?' he gave an almost girlish giggle, as if the notion were amusing to him.

'...It would then mean that we haven't entirely wasted our time in coming here,' Anton finished.

'Well,' he murmured, 'I suppose Allan might be able to give you the cook's tour... although it's quite irregular.'

'Who is this "Allan" please?' Anton pressed.

Tomlinson blinked. 'Strictly speaking, he's a member of the maintenance staff but, given our duties, our paths cross quite often. He was cashiered out of the army during the War—got badly wounded at Polygon Wood—and his role here allows him to work while taking into account his... limitations.'

Anton and I exchanged a glance.

'He's the closest you'll find to anyone around here who reports to me. His office is directly across the hall: tell him I asked if he could show you around a little. Now, I'm running late, and Sir Charles isn't a man to be kept waiting.'

He scooped up his ledgers once more and bustled off on his way but not before pointedly ensuring that we were outside his office.

Once the Reverend had disappeared from view, we sauntered across the corridor to the office over the way. Through the window in the door a light was visible, so Anton tapped briskly upon it with his cane. When no answer came, I tried the doorknob: the door was unlocked. I pushed it open and we looked inside.

Within, all was neat and tidy, illuminated by a brass desk-lamp atop a desk in the centre of the room. Banks of filing cabinets with tidily labelled drawers stood against the walls on all three sides of the room and a glass-fronted portrait of His Majesty hung from the wall opposite the door. The desk was topped by a blotter and inkstand and a small wooden tray held a neat assortment of stationery. A row of twelve leather volumes, their gilt-decorated spines facing the doorway, presented themselves to the visitor.

'May I help you, gentlemen?' A quiet voice surprised us from behind. Turning, we both took in a slight man in an Army uniform, leaning on a walking stick. He was mousey-haired with grey eyes behind circle-lensed spectacles and a neat moustache graced his upper lip. That he was pleased to see us was not something that could be read from his expression; rather, he seemed annoyed and radiated a sense that we were interrupting the well-ordered routine of a superior person. It seemed that he deliberately avoided making eye-contact with us, as if direct acknowledgement of our presence would only cause us to lengthen our stay. Anton took the lead.

'Are you Allan?' he chirped, 'My name is Anton Vadász and this is my associate Patrick Dolan. The Reverend told us that you might be able to guide us on a tour of the facility whilst he is otherwise engaged.'

The man's head jerked in the direction of the Chaplain's office and sharp notes of annoyance and displeasure flashed across his features. He switched his walking-stick from one hand to the other and ground it slowly onto the floor.

'Did he?' he muttered, the muscles in his jaw working, 'how typical of him.' He made a short motion with his free hand indicating that we should move out of his way and we followed his suggestion.

As he stepped forward and through the door into the office, the extent of his injuries became apparent. When he moved, he threw his right hip forward, forcing an inert right leg out in front of him. Then, using his good leg and the walking-stick, he hauled himself along behind, in a gait that suggested top-heaviness and an imminent collapse. He made his way laboriously around his desk, arm and shoulders jerking to maintain balance, and finally sank into his chair, clapping the cane across the blotter with a sharp note.

'I'm afraid, gentlemen,' he said in his quiet voice, 'That Reverend Tomlinson has rather overstepped his bounds. I am extremely busy and cannot take time from my schedule to accommodate you. And even if I could see my way to sparing you—and the good chaplain—a portion of my day, I certainly am not the ideal candidate to lead you on a walking tour of the facility.' From the way that acid dripped from this fellow's tone, I was sure that, wherever the chaplain was, his ears were burning.

Anton waved a dismissive hand. 'That's just as well,' he said brightly, 'we also have things that need our attention. But perhaps we could ask you a few quick questions before we leave you?'

Again, the stiff features broadcast displeasure and an unwillingness to stoop. 'Very well,' he seethed, 'I can spare you a few minutes.' He looked pointedly at his wristwatch.

I leaned against the edge of his desk and jerked my chin towards him. 'You get that from Jerry?' I asked.

He sat forward to lean on his elbows. Moving his cane so that it hung by its crook on the edge of the table, he said: 'A shell fragment shattered my pelvis during an attempt to storm a bunker while I was in Belgium. Is this question pertinent to your business?'

'Nope,' I shook my head, smiling, 'just making small talk.'

'Father Tomlinson mentioned that you worked on the maintenance staff,' Anton broke in, more or less throwing the chaplain to the wolves, 'can you tell me what it is that you do here?'

I could hear his teeth grinding a mile away.

'Technically,' he said, and the bitterness with which he admitted this was palpable, 'my functions fall within the purview of the maintenance staff; however, my duties range far beyond the simple administration of sanitation and building upkeep. Certainly, my situation doesn't allow me to climb ladders or fix roof tiles. In fact, since my role here is to see that condemned felons are processed with all duty and care, I have more in common with the Reverend Tomlinson than anyone else around this place, the difference being that he doesn't get his hands dirty!' Two patches of high colour had appeared in his pale cheeks.

'You're the hangman!' I burst out, sudden realisation kicking in.

He winced. 'I prefer my title, "Public Executioner", but yes, that's it in a nutshell.'

'I take it that you were present at the hanging of Eugene Lowell?' Anton asked.

'Yes. I processed him,' he said, 'a nasty piece of work, that one.'

'No doubt,' replied Anton, leaning his cane against his side of the desk and, sitting forward, idly running gloved fingers down the spine of one of the dozen volumes facing him. 'I assume that you arrange for the funerals of the condemned. Afterwards?'

Narrowed eyes gimleted at Anton. 'Occasionally, family comes to claim the body,' he said, 'if not, then the remains are buried in our own cemetery here at the gaol. In those instances, I work with the local undertaker in Brand to prepare things; but after that, well, you're in Reverend Tomlinson's bailiwick once more.'

'I take it then, that you are the one to encoffin the body?' Anton pressed.

Allan sighed, showing his annoyance. He drummed his fingers momentarily on the edge of the desk, then answered: 'The undertaker provides the casket which, as you'll expect, is of the most basic design. I telephone through the victim's height and weight and he then selects an appropriate container which is delivered to the prisoner's cell...'

'Surely, a box is a box, right?' I queried.

He smiled thinly, brushing away my ignorance with a brief hand gesture. 'You'd be surprised,' he said, 'caskets must be reinforced and lengthened to accommodate different occupants. The coffin I'd order for you, for example, would differ vastly from that which I'd obtain for your colleague here.'

'Huh,' I observed.

'Disposing of the condemned's *corpus* is no different from getting rid of the rest of his possessions,' he went on, 'everything in his cell is boxed up, or returned to the quartermaster for re-assignment, and yes,' his eyes flicked back at Anton once more, 'that task is my particular duty.'

'I see,' murmured Anton, 'and this graveyard for the condemned—is it far from here?'

'No,' he lurched suddenly to his feet, swaying precariously and steadying himself with a hand on his blotter, 'It forms part of the land acquired by the Government in order to build this new facility. Basically, it's just next door. Now gentlemen—is there anything else?'

Anton shook his head and stood up, snatching up his cane as he did so. 'I don't think so,' he said amiably extending his hand for shaking, 'however, we'll be coming back to see Reverend Tomlinson at a later stage—if I think of anything else, can I drop in and see you?'

Allan scowled as he shook Anton's gloved hand. 'I suppose...' he grudgingly conceded.

'*Apropos* of nothing,' Anton continued brightly, resting his fingertips on the books in front of him, 'these are fine volumes. Are they yours?'

'Um, yes,' he answered, 'that is, they belong to me.'

'Very nice,' Anton gushed, brushing the gilded leather and idly flicking a red bookmark sticking out of the top of one of the books, 'such a set must have cost you no few guineas...'

'Oh, they're an inheritance,' Allan objected, smiling, 'from my grandfather's estate. There's no way I could afford them on my stipend...'

'Well, I envy you your ownership of them. Come Patrick—let us occupy no more of Mr Quinlan's time. *Adieu!*' He tapped the name plate to the right of the books and turned briskly to the exit, stepping through into the corridor.

I stood up and touched the brim of my absent hat to the hangman. 'Quinlan, huh?' I said. 'I knew some Quinlans once. And Allan's your given name?'

He was fussing about with things on his desk, getting ready for his working day. 'It's actually Cecil,' he said offhandedly, 'but that was my father's name also, so I use my middle name to avoid confusion.'

'Gotcha,' I beamed, and showed him all my teeth. 'Well—see you later!'

'No doubt,' he growled as I stepped out after Anton.

Once the office door was shut behind me, I practically jogged after Anton, keen to reveal to him the information I had just discovered. However, he motioned me into silence.

'Yes,' he said, 'C.Q.—and this time I think we have it right. Did you notice the books?'

'I noticed that *you* did,' I answered, 'what about them?'

Anton turned and headed for the exit, speaking over his shoulder as he went. 'The primary sources for the culture associated with the Germanic peoples of Europe are Julius Caesar and a later historian named Tacitus. Without access to these works, and some facility with Latin, the next best option is Sir James Frazer's *The Golden Bough*, which gathers together much regarding folk beliefs, superstition and magic from across the world, including a reference to the ritual disembowelling of those who caused damage to notable trees. A copy of this work—in its current twelve-volume edition, dated 1915—is sitting, rather unexpectedly, on Allan Quinlan's desk.

I had seen this exact same set on display recently at Anthony Hordern's Emporium in Sydney and had thought to purchase it myself.'

'So not an inheritance, then?' I tapped a Red Capstan out of its packet.

'Not so much,' said Anton fiddling with his gloves before stepping outside, 'and the fact that he uses *kau li* as bookmarks provides a hint as to where he obtained the money to make such a purchase.'

'The *Resplendent Phoenix*!' I gasped; 'Then he *did* go back there with his widget, after racking-up his debt to *"Fan Tan"* Henry!'

'As you surmised,' agreed Anton, 'taking all the cash he could lay his hands on and also the *t'an pong*, with which he killed Mr Shi's partner.'

'That stick thing?'

'Precisely,' Anton looked out into the sun-dappled day that awaited us.

'We have to leave,' he said with some urgency 'and return to Potts Point. There is much to prepare, and we must start immediately.'

* * *

We went back to Anton's place and embarked upon a long series of telephone calls and telegrams to and from the Catholic diocese. I say "we", but this was all Anton's area of expertise—I spent most of the time sitting in the library with Anton's transcripts of the Hand of Glory recipes, listening to the tirade coming from Anton's office. It seemed like a Hell of a lot of effort to go to just to try and get some dead guy dug up.

At one point, while Anton was composing a diplomatic telegram to Sir Charles Quilter, the telephone in the front hall rang and I picked up the receiver.

'Vadász residence,' I said.

'Mr Dolan? It is Ji Daoyi speaking.'

'Hello Daoyi! How's Chinatown?'

'We are all well here,' he replied. 'I am calling to speak with Mr Vadász concerning Miss Shia Leiping and her remembrances of the attack upon the *House of the Jade Lotus*.'

'He's a little bit tied up at the moment,' I said, 'beating his head up against the Powers That Be. Let me know what you've got, and I can pass things along to him.'

'Very well. Leiping says that she was weary that evening and retired to the couch as soon as all the clients were seen to, and the guards had been fed and left to their *mah jongg*. She ate some food and then pulled the blanket over her head to try and sleep.'

'Sounds like what we expected,' I said, scribbling on a notepad next to the telephone.

'She says that she awoke to a loud crash,' Daoyi continued, 'she says that she heard some laughing and footsteps, like a drunken man walking about. She tried to cry out, but she found herself paralysed and unable to move. She told me that she had once seen the same effects from a type of poison in China and she thought that the food in the steamer had been corrupted by such means.'

'Reasonable assumption,' I muttered, scratching away.

'She said that the effect lasted for a very long time and she feared she would die, thinking soon the paralysis would stop her breathing. Later, she heard the drunken man approach once more and then she says she heard the front gate slamming. Some moments after this, she was suddenly able to move again. That is, when she found the murders and when she gathered up the opium and fled to the *Resplendent Phoenix.*'

'She's lucky to be alive,' I observed.

'Most certainly,' Daoyi said. 'I will call again if there is anything else to learn.'

'Right you are, Daoyi,' I said, 'See you later.' I rang off.

As I stood up and stretched, Tegbir materialised at the front door, after returning from the telegraph office. I ripped the page I had scribbled on from the notepad and handed it to him.

'Make sure Anton gets this, Tegbir,' I said, 'I'm going for a walk—I've spent too long inside today.'

He murmured a response through his magnificent beard and opened the cupboard which held our coats and hats when not in use. After slapping my fedora on my noggin, I stormed out into the late afternoon, eager for some exercise.

I ambled up Victoria Street amid the lengthening shadows and the smells of smoke from the dockyards. Gathering clouds spoke of a return of the rain and I turned my collar up against the weather's possibilities. I ducked up Orwell Street and stepped out into Macleay Street beyond that, turning right and heading into the 'Cross proper, to the intersection with William Street and Darlinghurst Road. The honey-gleam of the Empire Hotel's lights looked inviting, so I turned my steps in that direction—it was just a few minutes past five o'clock, so a legal drink was still a possibility. I was soon propped up against the bar with a schooner of beer; recognising a couple of Anton's journalistic buddies across the way, I raised my glass in recognition and took a sip.

I sat there with my thoughts for awhile, turning things over in my head. Since I had started working with Anton, I had seen some pretty weird things: people possessed by evil spirits; sorcerers swapping bodies; Hellhounds, for Christ's sake! Even Anton's Oldsmobile was strange enough, in its own way, to raise questions amongst the uninitiated. Now we were faced with this gruesome magical talisman, somehow made to work against all possible odds, and now being horribly utilised by its ruthless creator. With all of the various instructions for making this noxious object fresh in my mind, I felt my ability to accept Anton's rationalisation of the various clues we'd discovered fading away: wasn't it *simpler* to say that the food in the steamer had been poisoned? Wasn't it *easier* to assume that the murderer had been helped in his evil deeds by the fact that all the *Jade Lotus's* patrons had been intoxicated by opium?

I groaned and rubbed my forehead. Just trying to make a Hand of Glory was a gamble with long odds: some books said that the hand used in the spell must be the left hand of a hanged man; others made no such distinction. Most of the books described particular times of the year during which they had to be made; other were vague or dismissive, and that's before even considering the complexities of translating Northern hemisphere spellcraft into an antipodean jury-rig. All of the recipes had at least one ingredient that was unknown, or unclear, with only cautious guesses as to what they might possibly be. And after the thing was made, how did it work? Did it operate in only one dwelling? Could it only be extinguished with milk? Did it untie ropes as well as locks, and was this at the wielder's command, or an automatic effect? As Daoyi had pointed out, the way in which the object was supposed to work—quite apart from the possibility of creating it—was layered in speculation, mystery and supposition. The more I thought about it—and it certainly gave me the heebie-jeebies when I did—the more fantastic it seemed. And yet, here we were.

Around me, the pub had filled up with patrons, all bellied-up to the bar. It was a quarter to six and the Empire would shortly be required to stop selling booze. I figured I'd given Anton long enough to wind up whatever he was about, so I downed the dregs of my drink and pushed my way outside.

A tram clanged by as I crossed the street and turned left towards the top of Victoria Street. The air was thick with the metallic smoke of chimneys belching out towards Pyrmont, and the air hummed and zinged through the snarl of telegraph wires overhead. As the dark took hold, the gaslights bloomed into life, painting the cobblestones with gold.

Victoria Street was more subdued than King's Cross, darker yet more stately, with its elegant terraces and high-toned villas. In front of me, a dairy wagon trundled along the kerb, its horse clopping contentedly. I threw a cheery 'G'day!' to the driver and jogged ahead of it to the front gate of Anton's house. His catch-cry—*"Milk for the babies and cream for the ladies!"*—rang out behind me.

As I reached for the latch, the gate opened without me touching it. At the same instant, the front door and all the windows of the house gracefully unlocked themselves and swung wide, like some massive efflorescence opening up at the touch of the sun. I stood there gaping, with my jaw on the pavement.

Bewildered, I took a sudden step forward. As my arm crossed the property line, I felt it go dead, inert, and flop against my side. I arrested my forward movement and wheeled around to slam my back up against the front fence. Instantly my hand and forearm sang with pins and needles, painful and debilitating before fading away and restoring my arm to life once more. I suddenly knew what was happening: The Hand of Glory was showing its terrible power here, in Anton's house!

I scurried along the front fence of the block trying to see inside the building. It looked as though Tegbir had been turning on the lights with the approach of evening, but the illumination inside was far from revealing. Suddenly, I saw a flickering greenish glow coming from the French windows leading out onto the veranda. Through this window I could see Anton, sitting at the long table where he Daoyi and I had sat poring over transcripts a day or so ago. He had a black book open in his hand in an attitude as if he were bringing it up to his face for perusal but had been interrupted. Otherwise, he was as still and unmoving as a statue. There was another person in the room with him, dressed all in black and with a dark hood over his head; unlike Anton, he was moving freely, although clumsily.

On top of the table, emitting the weird light was a hideous object: it was a pale, human hand, shining with some waxy covering, standing upright on the stump of its wrist, the bluish veins showing through the withered skin. The smallest finger and the one next to it were charred, burnt away and covered with ash, the blackened bones of those ruined digits—those that were left—showing grotesquely. The central finger was wreathed with flickering greenish flame, slithering like an evil halo over the crackling flesh. Bubbling rivulets of greyish liquid oozed out and trickled down to the tabletop.

The moving figure in the room strode awkwardly around the table to a point behind Anton's chair. As it did so, it pulled a long blade out of its coat, single-edged with a quillon curled on one side—I saw at once that it was a standard-issue military bayonet. I grabbed the *fleur de lys* points of the fence iron before me in desperation. The dark figure moved between me and Anton and slowly raised its weapon...

"Ey, mate,' a voice sounded in my ear, 'these your digs? Just the usual, is it?'

Startled, I looked quickly sideways. Next to me, his horse and cart behind him, stood the milkman, holding out a lidded billy-can in my direction. In his other hand, he held a wooden carrier, rather like a toolbox, filled with five more pint tins palely shining in the gloom...

The milk crate crashed against the tabletop inside the house, cracking and sending the milk containers crashing in a shower of white foam. The Hand of Glory spun around on its horrible base and collapsed under a wave of white. For good measure, I grabbed the single billy out of the milko's hand and sent it in after the rest. Not waiting, I vaulted the fence and raced across the front garden to the veranda, noting with grim satisfaction that there was no sudden paralysing force to stop my progress. As I cleared the rosebushes, the windows and doors of the house all swung silently shut: I crashed up against the steel shutters of the French windows, finding them firmly locked once more.

'Oh, *come on!*' I shouted.

Scrabbling on the veranda tiles I struggled towards the front door and pounded on its inscrutable wooden surface, all the while pushing the button of the doorbell. I could hear the inane pealing of the bell deep within the structure. I kept pounding.

Suddenly the door flew open and Tegbir stood there, holding a hand to his turbaned forehead, a look of shock on his features. I grabbed him by the shoulders and shook him hard.

'Are you alright?' I yelled. He seemed dazed, but he nodded quickly.

I ducked past him into the library—clocking my head on that *damned* crocodile—and kept on running into the parlour beyond. Anton stood there, resting heavily against the table with one hand; around him there was a stark mess of white liquid and empty cans, dripping off the table edges and soaking into the carpet.

'Anton!' I cried, 'are you alright? Did that bastard hurt you?'

He turned his face to me, his eyes unfocussed, but a smile hovering on his lips.

'Patrick,' he said, 'you remembered the milk. So, all of that reading wasn't in vain...'

Then he slumped, senseless, to the floor.

'Hey!' a voice rang out angrily in the room behind me, 'who's gonna pay for those six pints?'

* * *

We got Anton to St. Vincent's in time, and an erstwhile doctor stitched him up and declared him good to go. He also said that Anton should stay longer for observation but, since we were being a bit parsimonious with the truth about how he came to be in this condition, they weren't pushing the issue—they get a lot of secretive types at St. Vincent's.

We put Anton in the back of the Oldsmobile, and I sat up front with Tegbir driving as we headed on back to Potts Point.

'You're sure it was him?' I asked over the back of my seat.

'As sure as I can be,' Anton replied.

'So why don't we just call the police?' I said, '"Kangaroo" Jack would more than happily pick up the collar...'

Anton waved a dismissive hand. 'We haven't anything to work with,' he said, 'nothing that can be used in a court of law...'

'But I saw him attack you!' I said.

'No,' Anton replied firmly, 'you saw *someone* attack me, an attack against which I did nothing to defend myself, in my open house, with my manservant in attendance. We'd be hard-pressed to even prove that what you saw *was* an attack...'

'But...!'

'No,' he said, 'this is for *us* to prosecute. The moment we raise the issue of a Hand of Glory in a courtroom, we'd be laughed right out of it. We'll have to proceed without the help of the Law.'

I turned around in my seat to face forwards once more. 'Alright,' I said, 'then what's next?'

He was silent for a bit. 'First, we need to go home—there's a book I need. Then we need to go to Long Bay...'

I turned once more to look at him, lying in the back seat. The passing streetlights lit him up then dropped him into darkness over and over.

'Are you alright?' I said.

He took a while to answer. 'It was terrible,' he said quietly, 'sitting there, watching my death approach at the hands of a maniac and not being able to do anything—*anything*—about it. I've never felt so helpless...'

'Never mind,' I said gruffly, 'we stopped him, despite his magical toy. Our team was best on the day...'

He nodded, then broke into a coughing fit. I reached around to help, but he raised his hand to stop me.

'I'm fine,' he said, 'I just need some rest, a few moments to gather myself before we end this...'

'Whatever you say, Anton,' I turned in my seat once more, cursing my inability to light a smoke. His words were reassuring, but the haunted look in his eyes was anything but...

* * *

Which brings us back to where we started—us, parked outside of Long Bay gaol, me dying for a cigarette and Anton reading his crazy books in the front seat. The last red light of sunset faded out of the sky and the cockatoos fell silent amongst the darkening trees.

I finished my smoke just as I heard Anton step out of the car. I skipped around to help him.

He struggled to exit so I lent him a hand. 'You up for this?'

He nodded, holding his side where his stitches were no doubt straining. I picked up the book that he'd been reading: the title page was all in Latin, but one word stood out from the pack of gibberish:

'*Daemonolatreia*?' I said, 'I remember—someone—told us that this was all so much horse feathers.'

Anton lifted the book from my hands. 'Its use is limited, in light of recent events,' he said, 'but there are still passages which retain their effectiveness.'

I shrugged and we headed off into the night, moving towards the prison cemetery.

The boundary was simply a low stone wall, curving out from the main body of the gaol and running along the drive leading from the front door. We stepped over this and moved among the headstones and other markers, relatively few in all. Soon, we stopped by a temporary sign and Anton played torch-light over it.

'Eugene Lowell,' he said.

He stepped back and took a deep breath, his eyes closed as he allowed the tension to drain from him. Then he began making small movements with his hands, muttering all the while. As we stood there, I heard a distant pattering sound approaching from the sea: rain coming, hammering through the gum leaves. As the first drops struck the ground around us, Anton pulled an old metal whistle from his pocket and blew a long, silent note upon it. Several dogs barked in the distance.

'*Ébren!*' he said aloud.

For a long heartbeat, nothing happened, and I began, quietly, to question the reputation of Remigius once more. Then Anton threw out an arm and moved both of us back towards the fence.

We heard a sudden series of harsh but muffled cracking sounds; then the surface of Eugene Lowell's grave began to stir. I noticed the turf over a number of the graves start to shift in a like fashion. Suddenly the ground opened, and several dead men groped their way upwards from the earth, hissing, long-stilled lungs filling with breath for the first time in ages, the dry leather of their flesh drumming woodenly under the raindrops. The air around us filled sharply with the stench of fetor. Soon, a half-dozen corpses—no longer content to lie still—stood before us, their stiffened joints cracking from unexpected use. Their heads turned slowly, as if taking in their surroundings, but few of them had eyes to see anything with. The other graves which hadn't disgorged their cadaverous loads, stirred with the motion of occupants unable to haul themselves free of the earth.

White light silvered the dead men standing before us and a burst of thunder crashed over the world.

Anton reached into a pocket and pulled forth a silken bag with a drawstring; this, he opened and pulled forth a pale object I recognised immediately: the Hand of Glory. As he raised it up, the creature that had once been Eugene Lowell stepped forward with a snarl, raising its arms: one of them was notable for the absence of its hand. Anton reached across and offered the talisman to its previous owner; the corpse snatched it and sped back to its coffin, digging down fiercely through the muddy soil to return to its grave, watching us over its shoulder as it did so. The other corpses gave vent to frustrated, inarticulate cries and lifted arms that carried few or no hands. Anton's gaze swept over them all.

'*Aludni!*' he commanded with a resigned gesture. Slowly, with obvious reluctance, the dead turned and began to dig themselves back to their rest.

We sat down on the low stone wall and I lit up a cigarette, handing it over to Anton, who held his hand to his side. He accepted it without a thought. Lighting another for myself, I squinted at him though the raindrops.

'Well?' I said.

'It's confirmation,' he said coughing gently, 'Quinlan's been experimenting for a while.'

I breathed smoke in two jets from my nostrils into the salty night air.

'Now what?' I asked.

Anton blew a cloud over his shoulder. His long black hair was plastered to his face and his eyes were unfocussed; unreadable.

'Now he pays for what he's done,' he said.

I stood up, my cigarette buzzing off into the night like an angry hornet. 'You leave that to me,' I said.

* * *

I caught up with Quinlan at the top of Bridge Street, catching a tram out to Bondi.

As I approached, I saw that the overhead cable had become detached from the tram and the conductor—a half-pint, clearly not up to the task—was flailing about with the tram hook, trying to get the cable back into position. I walked over to him.

'Let me give you a hand mate,' I said taking the tram hook out of his mitt. Reaching up, I tugged the cable back into place and tucked the hook under my arm while pulling out my wallet.

'Um, where to?' asked the conductor.

I jerked a thumb over my shoulder towards where Quinlan was seated. Squinting through the smoke of my cigarette, I said, 'Wherever he's going.'

'Bondi Junction it is,' he said, punching my ticket. He reached for the tram hook, but I rebuffed him.

'I'll just hang onto this for a sec', if you don't mind.' I jumped onboard and slid along the wooden seat next to my quarry.

He had his head buried in a copy of *The Sun*, his eyes glued to a page two article about grave-robbers outside Long Bay Men's Penitentiary in the Village of Brand.

'Bad business, that,' I observed.

He almost jumped out of his skin. His eyes widened in horror behind his spectacles and he paled perceptibly. With a clang of bells, the tram sped away up Bridge Street, rattling and swaying. I rested my hand on Quinlan's shoulder.

'Heading to the surf, hey?' I said, 'bit late for a swim, but never mind.'

His eyes darted all over the place, looking for an exit. I tightened my grip.

'I wouldn't try it if I were you,' I said, 'cripple like you could do himself an injury...'

'I am not a cripple!' he hissed, anger rising in his face.

'Sure, you're not,' I smiled, showing all my teeth, 'and my great-aunt Mildred's a taxi-dancer in a burlesque house. Ooh—did I touch a nerve?' He struggled under my paw.

'Just for nothin', Quinlan' said leaning close, 'If you're carrying that bayonet under your coat, you try and reach for it, and you won't enjoy what happens next.' I let the tram hook fall gently to rest on the back of the seat in front of us. He stopped moving, but he was still tensed up. We travelled along in silence for a bit.

'Cigarette?' I offered. He shook his head. I shrugged and lit one for myself.

'Y'know,' I said, 'your problem is pride. That's where you go wrong.'

He snorted derision. 'Is it?' he said. 'That's your diagnosis?'

I nodded taking a deep draw on my smoke. 'Raised by priests,' I explained; 'you pick up a thing or two.' I swivelled around in the seat to face him. 'Where you went wrong,' I continued, 'is in thinking everyone else is out to get you; that this

is all some kind of contest and you have to be the one on top.'
I waved my hand to indicate the world in general.

'*"Fan Tan"* Henry?' I continued, pointing my smoke at him, 'You got in hock with him and you thought he *made* you walk into his joint and lay your hard-earned on the drumhead. All he was thinking was "come in y'mug—give it your best shot". You thought there's no way a bloke from China could be smarter than you, but guess what? You found out the hard way.'

I watched his jaw muscles tighten beneath his pallor.

'You showed *him* though, didn't you?'

The derisive snort again, this time with a slow smile.

'Your *big* mistake though,' I went on, 'was trying to take on Anton Vadász. Now, *you* might think you're smart, but he's way ahead of you, son. You're not even playing the same game.'

Quinlan's hands clenched into fists in his lap.

'In fact, while we're having this nice little chat, he's tearing apart your office down in Long Bay, collecting all your notes and such before someone else tries your little experiment.'

He lurched up in his seat again, groping for the stop signal. I grabbed his shoulder and slammed him down on the bench once more.

'Easy, son,' I smiled, 'your stop's up ahead. And don't worry—he'll take good care of those fancy books of yours.'

He gripped the back of the seat in front of him, his knuckles turning white. His newspaper slid off his lap and fell into the street, where it blew away in the night. The tram bell clanged once again, and the conductor announced the end of the line.

As we came to a halt, I slid out onto the road, dragging Quinlan with me. I threw him roughly against the side of the tram where he gasped. He fumbled rapidly with his coat and lifted the pigsticker; I slapped it out of his hands and it flew off into the darkness, clanging dismally off the tarmac.

'What'd I tell you, Quinlan?' I said leaning close, 'apparently, your other problem is you don't listen well.'

He broke away from me, staggering awkwardly along the tram's chassis, using it for support, his teeth chattering.

'Good idea, Quinlan,' I called after him, 'you might find a cab over that way, just watch out for the—'

He fell down suddenly, with a scream.

'—the tramlines,' I finished. I lit another smoke and hefted the tram hook.

When I caught up with him, he was lying on his back on the road. The ankle of his good foot was twisted strangely and there was blood on his sock. He was shivering and waving his hand at me, trying to conjure me away. I pointed the tram hook at him, and he flinched, closing his eyes.

'No, mate,' I said around my smoke, 'you'll keep your eyes *open*. You need to watch all of this.'

And he did.

Right 'til the end.

IV.

"BOX OF LUCIFER"

BOX OF LUCIFER

---

*"HE WHO HAS REJECTED HIS DEMONS, BADGERS US
TO DEATH WITH HIS ANGELS"*

- HENRI MICHAUX

Barnabas Hubble struggled out of his bed, pushing aside the books that covered his blanket—dog-eared, open and face-down. Never a morning lark, Barnabas shuffled, dressing-gown clad, from the humid fug of unwashed sheets to the crockery clutter of the kitchen sink. The least repulsive cup soon brimmed with an infusion of yesterday's tea leaves, re-heated for a new dawn, several mouthfuls of which bolstered him to face the lunge outside to collect the morning 'paper from the passing newsboy...

The only thing of interest to Barnabas in the daily rag was the horse racing news. The form guide was soon spread across the kitchen table, held down by the lukewarm teacup and the daily apparatus of Barnabas's musings: a ruler; a charcoal pencil; five Chinese coins; a pack of tarot cards and a pendulum. First, he reviewed the horse's names, looking for anything auspicious. Of those that caught his eye, he performed some quick *gematria*, converting names to numbers and calculating numerological possibilities. He checked likely candidates by their alignment to each other on the page, then turned tarot cards and consulted the *I Ching* for the jockeys listed. Finally, he hovered over the remaining handful with his pendulum, minutely observing its oscillations...

With this shortlist of betting options, Barnabas then turned to his well-thumbed copy of *"Zophiel's Antipodean Astrological Almanac"* and looked up the day's entry:

"A steady routine will go off the rails today—look out for surprise evening visitors! Minor facial injuries."

Barnabas wrinkled his brow and contemplated the hidden aspects of the message while slurping cold tea. He wasn't a fan of this astrological writer, but she was better—to his mind—than her peers who produced similar star guides. His research gave her better than even odds in accuracy on most days, even though her allusions were occasionally a little off-point, or syrupy. He tucked her predictions in the back of his mind and began preparations for the day ahead.

It went badly. The sky was overcast, and the track was heavy—because he'd failed to take into account a significant Water-Earth conjunction, several of his bets were pipped at the post. One jockey was replaced at the last minute by an attack of appendicitis, thus ruining his delicately balanced prognostications. Of his six picks, only two came through, but these had come late in the day when his confidence was shot, and he'd wagered only cautious amounts. Leaning on the track-side rail in the afternoon drizzle, with a paper cup of cold, milky tea, he resigned himself to a night at the dog-races to make up the deficit in his rent.

Evening found him in the stands under the lights, huddled in his threadbare coat with a cooling meat pie in each hand, the greasiness of their dubious contents causing his stomach to groan in protest. On the seat beside him lay a pack of playing cards, a racing guide, a pencil and his pendulum. He hated the dog races: they were too unpredictable; things switched too quickly; they made too much noise and ruined his concentration. All his predictions had to be done on the fly with less-than-perfect data. Nevertheless, by the end of the meeting, he was only a couple of shillings short of his target. He kicked his way through the discarded betting slips on the way out, eagle-eyed for the possibility of dropped change.

By the time he got home he was damp and tired, and his belly complained about its meal of rat coffins. He moped through the wet air in his flat, picking listlessly at the piles of newspapers and the washing-up, a-scuttle with cockroaches in the sink. He tried going to bed, but his track-side meal weighed on him like a stone. Finally, he decided to take a bath and shave.

Thus it was that, when the Archangel Michael kicked in his front door, he nicked himself with his razor before launching himself through the bathroom's small window and down into the alley below...

* * *

This, anyway, is what he told me when we met at the Criterion Hotel in Newtown.

'How do you know it was the Archangel Michael?' I asked him.

Barney shrugged. 'Wings. Halo. Massive sword: it's fairly easy to spot him.'

Hubble's drinking mate, Blind Bert, rotated his schooner carefully on its bar mat. He had one ear tuned into the racing results being announced by the SP Bookie stationed at the end of the main bar, while the other was listening to Barney's querulous tale. Being blind as a rock allowed Bert to divide his attention in this fashion quite readily.

'So, you threw yourself through a window at the first sign of an angel,' he said. 'Given your peccadilloes, wouldn't it have been better to stick around and have a bit of a chinwag?'

Barnabas shook his head, then said "no", because Bert needed the version accompanied by dialogue.

'Angels are *implacable*, Bert,' he said, 'they have *missions* and they don't let anything, or anyone, get in their road. Whatever he was doing there, I didn't want any part of it. He'd probably prefer to lop my head off rather than discuss the damage he'd just done to my front door...' He stopped.

'Bloody Hell,' he went on, realisation dawning, 'my door...'

As we sat there, a kid, well under the legal drinking age, ran through the door and rushed over to the bookie, whispering hurriedly in his ear.

'Bugger!' spat Bert, eavesdropping, and tore up his betting slip while the bookmaker started a flurry of erasing and chalk-marking on his easel-propped blackboard in the background. Bert reached forward tentatively with one hand and patted Barnabas's shoulder after locating it.

'Never mind,' he soothed, 'it's just a door. *They* can be mended—heads can't. Hang on a mo...' He lurched to his feet and tapped his way over to the bookie.

I tossed a cigarette into my mouth and lit it with a match, popped on my thumbnail.

'Any idea why the Archangel Michael would be trying to track you down?'

Barney scratched his Brylcreemed head trying to think. He was an unprepossessing kind of fellow, with watery-blue pop-eyes, and a minimum quantity of chin beneath a gap-toothed overbite. He wore a shiny, hand-me-down black suit that had been painstakingly embroidered all over in black thread—if you looked closely enough, it fashioned the sorts of circles and other magical diagrams which abounded in the library of my associate Anton Vadász. He was without hat and collar—apparently his escape from the Archangel didn't allow time for the niceties of public attire. He spread his hands wide in surrender.

'I have no idea...' he said.

I blew smoke away from him, squinting.

'Would it maybe have something to do with "not suffering a witch to live"?' I asked.

He threw himself back in his chair. 'Witches were an obsession of James Stuart; *that* idea was added to his version of the Bible to curry favour. It's a fairly recent innovation...'

'Recent, huh?'

'...in the grander scheme of things. Archangels have been around since the dawn of time.'

I tapped my smoke over the nearby ashtray. 'So whaddaya want *me* to do about this?'

'This is your area of expertise, isn't it?' he wheedled, 'you deal with this kind of thing all the time, don't you?'

'Demons; sorcerers; Hell-hounds—that's what I'm usually called upon to deal with. I've not messed about with the other side of the street before and, I'm thinkin', maybe I shouldn't start now...'

Barney leant forward again. 'But this isn't *fair*; I've done *nothing!*'

I crushed out my smoke. '...that you're aware of,' I interjected. 'From what I've been told, "fair" doesn't usually come into it. And angels aren't the types to make mistakes.' I leaned in close. 'What've you been up to? I mean, what kinds of powers are you playing with that would garner you this kind of attention?'

Barney shrugged elaborately, throwing me a bewildered look. 'I'm strictly junior division,' he said. 'Casting horoscopes; working the Cabbala. I sling the pasteboards; dabble with some *I Ching*—but that's about it. Nothing with any real juice.'

'What's "eetching"?' I asked.

He groaned. 'Chinese astrology and fortune-telling?' he summarised. 'Are you *sure* you're up to this?'

'We'll see,' I grinned. 'Don't you have some way of working out where the Archangel Michael is going to show up, so that you can simply avoid him?'

He drummed his hands gently on the table. 'You mean like scrying for him?'

I threw an open-handed gesture at him. 'If you like,' I said.

He stared off into the middle distance, pinching his lower lip and considering. 'It's...possible,' he said hesitantly; 'it *could* work...' He reached into his jacket and fumbled with an inner pocket, pulling forth a much-handled, printed pamphlet, the wrappers of which were decorated with a bunch of mystic sigils. He flipped it open and began poring through the contents.

'What's that?' I asked warily. My experience of these sorts of booklets has not been particularly positive.

'The "*Poule Noire*",' he said scanning and flipping pages, 'it's a potent grimoire.' His eyes flicked up at me as if in challenge.

I was fumbling through my school French. 'Doesn't that mean... "black chicken"?' I said.

'It's just a name; the reasons behind it are lost to time,' he said, putting the book down and spreading it out flat, 'but it works. Here we go.' He leaned close, muttering the words under his breath.

'I've got it, now.' He straightened up, squinting, 'All I need now, is a vessel of water to see into...'

I slid Bert's abandoned beer across the table and stopped it in front of him, quirking my eyebrows and smiling at him around my smoke.

He shook his head, ruefully. 'Needs must, I suppose...'

He sat forward and placed a hand on the tabletop on each side of the glass. Light from the busy street outside sent golden rays through the amber liquid, making it glow and swim with shadows. He closed his eyes and murmured. Then, he stared intently down into the glass's unplumbed depths.

'Show me...' he breathed.

I scraped my chair around to sit beside him and peered down into the glowing beverage as well.

A haze in the depths of the amber fluid became a shadow, and that shadow grew, spreading out and taking form. The image coalesced into the shape of a gigantic man, golden of skin and hair, lantern-jawed with a severe mouth and a determined gaze that brooked no refusal. The eyes were two blank metallic orbs. Barnabas leaned closer, trying not to lose his concentration.

'Why is he upside-down?' I asked.

A massive golden hand descended on top of the glass and crushed it into a splintered puddle on the tabletop. Barnabas and I jerked backwards in our seats and stared up at the scowling metallic face looming over us. With casual ease, the aureate arm swept the table away from in front of us to shatter into so much kindling against the pub wall.

'*Run!*' I yelled, grabbing Barney by the collarless scruff. We tripped over our chairs rushing to get out of range. Barney finally got his feet to catch up with current events at about the same time that I rolled across the sticky carpet to get clear.

A burst of yellow light and a blast of heat followed right on my heels.

Clambering upwards, I saw Barney fling open the door to the gent's room, completely ignoring the door right next to it with the word "Exit" clearly emblazoned. He scurried inside like a mouse heading for a hole in a skirting board with a cat on its heels.

Another explosion picked me up off my knees and tossed me across the room. I vaulted some tables and threw my back against the gent's room door: the front of the hotel, where we'd been sitting, was in flames and the façade of the building seemed to have been torn right off. The golden figure was striding through the carnage, brushing furniture and patrons aside like they weren't even there.

'Bloody Hell!' I managed to say before pushing the door in and following in Barney's tracks.

I found him in one of the stalls, desperately trying to kick out the window that pierced the wall behind the cistern downspout.

'Barney!' I yelled, finding my coat on fire and shrugging out of it, 'that's not gunna work!'

His face, as he looked back at me, was a mask of terror, wide-eyed with gap-teeth bared. He thumped at the glass and smashed it; then he began beating at the pipe that prevented him from gaining access.

'Barney!' I tried again, 'it's too small!'

'For you maybe,' he shrieked through chattering teeth.

Around me, yellow light was growing in intensity. I swung around and raised my fists; the edges of the door we'd come in by were streaming with light. I heard the pipe crack and water gushed to the floor soaking my feet; then the door flew off its hinges and crashed into me.

It was the last thing I remembered.

* * *

They pulled me out from under a pile of broken bricks and tiles in the alley behind the Criterion. Bad as the place looked from there, it was worse out front. Fire had swept through the main bar and the façade of the building had been blackened with flame. I watched it slide by from inside the ambulance that carried me to St. Vincent's Hospital.

They strapped me up pretty good and gave me some stuff to keep the throbbing at bay. I checked myself out as soon as was decent and made my way to Anton's place in Potts Point.

Tegbir, Anton's taciturn Sikh manservant, met me at the front door. He took one look at the condition I was in and hustled me through to the main parlour where he deposited me in an armchair with a blanket and a snifter of brandy.

He poked at me with deft fingers, his eyes frowning below his burgundy turban.

'The arm is broken?' he asked.

I shook my head. 'Nah. Just sprained the wrist. I forgot keep my arm straight while trying to punch the flying masonry.'

He tut-tutted and pulled my head 'round by the chin to look at my temple.

'This is not good,' he summarised. 'And the ribs are broken?'

'No, just cracked.'

He stood up. 'Rest,' he said, 'I will prepare something to help.' Then he shimmered off to get his boss.

Anton perched on a straight-backed chair while I told him my tale of woe. He sat with his eyes closed behind his steel-rimmed spectacles, frowning underneath his widow's peak. When I'd finished, he removed his glasses, pinched the bridge of his aquiline nose and sat back, smoothing down his quilted, scarlet smoking-jacket.

'I believe, Patrick,' he sighed, 'that you have had a very narrow escape.'

I snorted. 'You think? He wasn't exactly handing out hugs, y'know!'

He smiled, 'Certainly. And yet, here you are, indicating that, whatever it was that was the object of its pursuit, it wasn't you. Otherwise, things would have ended quite differently.'

'"It"?' I queried.

Anton waved a hand. 'Angels; demons; devils—they're not human, Patrick, although efforts have been made to make them appear so. An angel is to a human being as a human being is to a microbe—an annoyance, if regarded at all. What you call "Michael" is more force than entity, and your choice of pronouns blinds you to that fact.'

I rubbed my forehead. 'When I was at school, they always told us that angels were the good blokes; that you could *trust* them; *pray* to them, for Chrissake! And this one drops down and goes through us like a dose of salts. What's he—*it*—playing at?'

Anton shrugged and twirled his glasses by their earpiece. 'That,' he stated, 'is the crucial question. Did this Barnabas Hubble fellow tell you why the Archangel attacked him?'

I shook my head and eased back into my chair, wincing. 'We didn't get that far into it. It seems he's just a dabbler, using astrology and scrying to pick the ponies in the horse races...'

'A hedge-witch?'

'If you like.' I took a swig of brandy. 'He had a grimoire, called the Black Chook...'

'"*La Poule Noire*"!'

'That's what I said—' but Anton had sprinted off into his library. He appeared some minutes later with a number of slim, leather-bound volumes, one of which he flipped open to the title page and held out to me.

'Does this look familiar?' he asked.

I took the book and squinted at it through my good eye. 'Yep,' I said, 'that's seems like it. His was just paper though...'

'Not surprising,' Anton sat back down again, placing the books on the long table that ran the length of the room. 'Like the *Petit Albert*, or *Le Dragon Rouge*, these chapbooks are produced cheaply, copied whole, or in part, and added to from other sources. Wherever Mr Hubble's copy came from, it must have additional elements within it that make it particularly puissant.'

'Why "Black Chicken", though?'

Anton crossed his legs at the ankles and smiled wryly. 'The book is supposed to have been narrated to a French soldier, saved from an Arab attack by an ancient Turk, who spirited him away to the interior of a pyramid. There, he tutored him in a range of ancient spells, the purpose of which was to acquire great wealth.'

'Sounds dodgy to me,' I scoffed.

Anton waved a dismissive hand. 'I agree—the notion is likely spurious. The signature spell within the grimoire is one which uses a black hen to summon a spirit, or genius, which will then transform the bird such that it will lay eggs of gold. Thus, "*Poule Noire*".'

I stared at Anton for a moment then broke out laughing, stopping only because it hurt my ribs so much.

'And people *believe* this rubbish?' I rubbed my side ruefully.

Anton smiled. 'As I said, these grimoires are primarily a means of separating the gullible from their money, not works of great respectability, or truth. This one, however, might have had something added to it, something that *actually* works; something that an angel might want to retrieve—or destroy.'

I leant my head back, closing my eyes and trying to relax all the bits that ached.

'What's the plan, Anton?' I breathed. 'How do we start?'

He smiled at me slowly. 'Why don't we take a leaf out of Mr Hubble's book?' he said.

* * *

The Oldsmobile purred to a stop outside the Museum on College Street. Tegbir hauled on the brake while Anton peered through the windows, looking out into the night beyond. In one hand he held a pendulum, hovering over a map of the middle of Town which rested in his lap. In the back, I sprawled across the bench seat, groaning with every lurch and shake of the car. Tegbir had changed my bandages and filled me up with some foul-tasting decoction that dulled the pain, but I still felt justified in whingeing.

'We're close.' Anton pushed open the door and stepped out onto the kerb. Tegbir helped me to struggle out, mindful of my ribs and various other contusions and sprains. Once we were all set, he pulled a lantern out of the boot and we took stock. I lit up a smoke.

'What have you got on under your coat, Tegbir?' I asked. I patted his shoulder, feeling stiff resistance underneath the outer fabric.

His eyes, the only bit of his face I could really make out in the dark between his turban and his beard, flashed at me.

'It is a coat of mail, Mr Dolan,' he said matter-of-factly. Reaching into the front seat of the car, he pulled out a long, curved sword in its scabbard.

I breathed smoke. 'You think things will get that bad?' I asked.

'*"No one is saved by mere talk and speech, nor by the reading of many books,"*' he said, strapping on his pigsticker. 'That is wisdom from *my* holy book, Mr Dolan.'

'Fair enough,' I said.

'That way.' Anton pointed in the direction of the Harbour.

We trudged along the footpath that bounded this side of Hyde Park. Construction work had torn up the flagstones in several places, so we dodged a couple of muddy, treacherous patches. Across the street, the stern face of the Museum loomed over us, its many windows shining in the moonlight. We paused on the corner of Park Street and Anton fiddled with his pendulum once more.

'There,' he said, pointing ahead. His gesture indicated the long, dark bulk of St. Mary's Cathedral.

'You can't be serious!' I scoffed.

Anton tucked his scrying equipment into his coat pocket. 'It makes sense, when you think about it,' he said. 'An angel's certainly not going to do anything untoward on consecrated ground. At least, I assume that is the trend of Mr Hubble's thinking.'

'That doesn't sound very definite,' I muttered, ashing my cigarette.

'When is it ever?' Anton flashed another smile and stepped off into the street, angling for the Cathedral and the construction site on its doorstep.

St. Mary's had been under construction since the late 1800s and, throughout the Catholic community of the City, there were constant calls and cash collections to get it finished off before the next big Vatican event took place. All through my school years, we had been dragged out to see the consecration of this or that, along with the installation of various relics. At this point, the nave still hadn't been completed and, as for the two southern bell towers, it was anyone's guess as to when they'd be finished.

For now, construction on the cathedral was at a standstill, but the worksite, bounded around with tall wooden fences, made a massive eyesore on its front doorstep. Anton stood against this barrier and waited for us to catch up: without

Tegbir's assistance, I wasn't hurrying anywhere. Once across, we shuffled along the street to the western side of the edifice.

A flight of wide stone steps led up to the side entrance into the transept and I limped up these with Tegbir's aid. By the time we reached the massive doors, Anton had made short work of the lock and had pulled the door open a few inches, peering into the gloom inside.

'I thought churches weren't supposed to be locked,' I muttered.

Anton shrugged. 'Not in this town,' he said.

'Right,' I conceded, 'wouldn't do to have anyone trying to claim Sanctuary after hours, right?' I flicked my cigarette away into the darkness towards the street. Up above the swaying mass of trees that covered Hyde Park in a shifting blanket of night, lightning shivered through the sky overhead. I looked up to see grasping fingers of cloud fall upon the moon and tear it from view.

'Bonzer!' I breathed. We crept inside.

The place smelt of damp stone, wilting flowers, old incense and shadows. There were several long benches in front of us, topped with hymnals and vases of lilies. Beyond these, the vast interior of the cathedral proper extended.

The space was immense, felt rather than seen, but dark and smothering, despite the sense of a huge soaring void overhead. Beams of silvered light drifted through from the windows behind us, revealing strange sections of columns, patches of flagstone and clusters of pews. An echo of lightning from outside shimmered on the meniscus of the font next to where I was standing: I dipped two fingers into the water and made the sign of the cross.

'What is that over there?' Tegbir gestured forwards with his lantern.

Ahead of us, amid an arrangement of pews at the point where the two corridors of the cathedral intersected, was a small flickering patch of yellow light. Illuminated by this glow, was a trousered leg and a shoe which had seen better days. A snore ripped out, echoing in the cold stone space.

'I'm guessing that's Barney,' I sighed.

We shuffled our way over to him. He was lying asleep on the floor between two pews, covered in his coat and surrounded by cards, coins with their centres punched out, and scraps of notepaper. A gathering of wax tapers made a molten mess on the seat above him. I reached forward and pinched these wicks out—the cathedral had burnt down twice already since building had begun; I didn't want that happening again if I could avoid it.

'Aha!' Anton reached quickly forward and snaffled Barney's open and face-down copy of *La Poule Noire* from where it threatened to become a permanent feature of the seating by virtue of being drowned in melted wax. He held it up into the light and then moved a short distance away to sit down, flicking through the pages and musing.

'Wha—?' Barney came awake suddenly and smacked his forehead on the underside of the bench he was lying beneath. 'Ow!' he groaned.

'G'day Barney,' I grinned down at him around an unlit cigarette, 'watcha doin'?'

He stared at me like I was a ghost. 'You're alive!' he gasped.

'No thanks to you,' I sneered, 'it seems your angel buddy was less interested in *me* than he was in *you*.'

He struggled to his feet and stepped out into the aisle that led to the altar. After a sudden glance at the pew he'd been hidden under, he blanched and started patting all his pockets. He stopped when he saw Anton across the way, reading the grimoire. Anton said nothing but raised the booklet momentarily showing Barney the cover; then he bent his head and continued reading.

'Potent stuff that,' I said. 'Probably meant for more significant things than just picking a winner on the gee-gees though, don'tcha think?'

'I-I didn't really comprehend the subtleties of it,' he stammered, 'It was just supposed to be some handy ways to get rich...'

'Easy money?'

He nodded. Spotting my unlit durry, he said. 'You got a spare one of those?'

I scoffed. 'Even if I did Barney, what makes you think I'd let you light up in a church? Besides, Michael set fire to my matches back at the Criterion, and I haven't had the opportunity to get some more.'

'Oh!' Barney fumbled in his waistcoat pocket: 'here—take mine. I owe you—it's the least... the least I can do.' He slapped a matchbox into my palm and stepped back, cringing.

Narrowing my eyes at him, I held the box to my ear and gave it a shake: it rattled in that silky-brittle way a full box of matches should.

'Thanks, Barn'' I said, 'but—like I said—no smoking 'til we're out of here.'

He breathed out heavily, his shoulders slumping, and nodded rapidly. His forehead glistened with sweat in the half-light.

'Right,' I turned to Anton, 'how're we going? Can we get out of here now?'

Anton raised a finger sharply and his gimlet gaze swivelled to lock onto Barney, who was shrugging into his intensely embroidered coat.

'I think we have a problem,' he said.

A play of red-gold beams flashed in though the western windows and a heavy boom broke the silence from outside. An unsteady candelabra standing against the far wall vibrated slightly, tapping an unsteady foot on the cold stone floor.

'What the Hell was that?' I asked. The only response I got was the sound of Barney's footsteps echoing away towards the altar.

'Bugger!' I breathed.

Anton leapt to his feet. 'Leave him to me,' he snapped, 'you two need to stay here.'

'What's up Anton?' I asked.

He raised the grimoire. 'As I suspected, this is a typical version of *La Poule Noire*; however, it has been extensively added-to. There are selections here from the *Clavicula Salomonis* and, possibly, the *Pope Honorius* too, mostly incomplete as far as I can surmise.' He was digging in his pocket—his hand drew forth a couple of sticks of white chalk.

'And what does that mean?'

'It's *goetia*, Patrick,' he continued, as if a gibberish word like "go-ay-sha" explained everything. 'This is no longer just a cheap swindle playing on the greed of the benighted. It contains material to summon and bind supernatural entities.'

I plucked my smoke from my lips, wishing to Hell that it was lit. 'Like the Archangel Michael, you mean?'

'Worse,' he said, 'this grimoire contains a spell to summon the Devil himself. I think that's why Michael is here—to undo something incredibly foolish that Barney has done.'

There was a moment while all of this sank in.

'Where is that little weasel,' I growled, 'I'm gunna—!'

'Leave him to me,' repeated Anton, 'I'm hoping that the entity Michael will be unwilling to unleash its full power here on consecrated ground. In that sense, it should be less likely to attack you here...'

'"Should"?'

'Nothing's certain with this type of thing, Patrick, as I said earlier. Stay here and defend yourselves!' He fled away towards the apse in pursuit of his quarry.

'Alright, Tegbir,' I said, turning to him, 'let's see what we can do about barricading those doors—'

But we were no longer alone. Standing behind Tegbir was a superhumanly tall, dark individual, but how he'd managed to get there without either of us noticing, I couldn't say. The face was the same as the one I'd clocked at the Criterion Hotel, but the presentation was different: his hair was short and slicked back, and he wore a tidy, three-piece suit, eerily reminiscent of Barney Hubble's wardrobe, right down to the elaborate embroidery and the missing collar. With his dead-gold eyes locked onto me, he picked Tegbir up by the scruff with one hand and tossed him over his shoulder, like a society matron disposing of an unwanted scatter cushion. The manservant slammed into a distant column and fell down into the darkness with a crash.

My old boxing coach always told me that, in a fight, you need to take opportunities where you found them and strike when your opponent was off-balance. Accordingly, while

Michael was finding his footing again after this casual assault, I slammed my fist up into his solar plexus with every ounce of force I could muster. I occasionally kid myself that he might've even felt it.

I ended up on the flagstones thirty feet away, aching from a dozen places and watching him stride implacably over towards me, with a view to finishing what he'd started. I struggled to get upright, but a shrill pain sang through my arm: my elbow had shifted to an odd angle and a slow red stain spread through my coat sleeve. I groaned: above me, the golden face of the angel drew near, silver light flickering across it from the lightning outside.

With a sudden, sharp cry, Tegbir leapt out of the gloom swinging a shimmering length of metal. He crashed into the angel, planting a foot in its chest and slamming the pommel of his sword down on top of its head before rolling off to land on his feet like a cat, between me and our foe. In response, there was a flurry of limbs and Tegbir was airborne once more, this time slamming into the wall on the opposite side of the transept with a ringing crash.

A hand grabbed my shoulder and shook hard.

'Get up!' Anton urged, 'this way. Quickly!'

I struggled to my feet, holding my broken arm close against my side, and lurched in the direction he was dragging me. As we staggered towards the altar, I could feel the angel getting closer by the rising of the temperature at my back. I was filled with a sinking feeling of despair; I was too frightened to even look back in case of what I might see.

Anton let go of me at the bottom of the three steps that led up into the apse and my knees turned to jelly beneath me. I fell to the floor. 'Stay here,' he ordered and stepped back towards the angel, unsheathing his sword-cane.

I rolled onto my back, lifted my head and stared. The angel strode across the transept, barefoot but still wearing its modern suit which crawled with mystical black symbols. As it approached, flames uncurled about it in a flickering halo, whirling like fire in a tornado and spiralling up into two long jets, billowing off either shoulder. It bore down upon Anton who was thrown into silhouette before it. The sheer rage emanating from this colossus was palpable and spelt nothing good for my friend.

Suddenly Anton threw his arms wide to either side, his sword-point raised to the roof.

'*Set etiam!*' he cried.

A pale white light flared across the floor and traced a series of sweeping lines inscribed there. The angel came to a sudden halt in the centre of this glowing matrix. It felt like a train crashing into a buffer at full speed a few inches away. It tottered momentarily, then opened its mouth to scream: the sound that bellowed forth was like all the eagles in the world giving voice at once and dragged claws through my soul. I figured, if it was mad before, now we'd really ticked it off.

The whirling halo of flame went berserk, spinning around the creature like a pillar of fire. When it died down, the angel had returned to the form in which I'd first encountered him—a huge, long-haired naked man with a sword of jetting flames. It roared down at Anton, heat rolling across the floor to wash over us.

'Patrick!' Anton called over his shoulder through gritted teeth, 'please come here!'

I staggered to my feet and, like a man pushing through a hurricane, hobbled over to stand next to him. He was shivering like he had a fever and sweat was pouring off him.

'I –I can't keep this up for long!' he gasped. 'We must work quickly!'

'Whaddaya want me to do?' I yelled above the din.

'Get—get the grimoire from my coat pocket,' he ordered, 'and put it on the floor in front of me!'

I stuck my unlit smoke between my lips and patted Anton down. The book was in his left-hand pocket, so I hooked it out and slapped it down on the floor.

'N-now, take out the matchbox I saw Mr Hubble give to you,' Anton's eyes had begun to lose focus.

'Right,' I said reaching into my pocket, 'you think burning this rag will set things straight?'

'*Don't open it!*' Anton was about as frantic as I'd ever seen him. 'Just put it down on the grimoire and step back!'

I plucked forth the matches that Barney had given me and looked at them. They looked like your typical box of lucifers that you'd get from any kiosk, but I suddenly noticed something: the box was decorated all over with a series of symbols, seemingly created using red sealing wax. On one side was a circular pattern with a star inside it and, on the other, a less formal design that resembled a clawed hand holding a pitchfork. The angel's firelight slid seductively over the waxy lines. I shook it and that silky rattle now sounded like a snake-pit in full seethe. Sudden frost shot through my body dulling all my pain in a rush of terror. I dropped the box onto the chapbook and almost fell over with fright trying to get away from it. I cringed behind Anton.

'What the Hell do we do now?' I yelled, trying to be heard over the firestorm.

'Who knows?' he screamed in reply. 'I'm—I'm going to drop this. I just hope that the angel will take the offering and leave us be.' He had started to shake uncontrollably from the effort, so I grabbed him and tried to prop him up.

'Let's—let's move back a step,' he cried.

I dragged him back towards the altar and the white light from the sigils he'd drawn on the floor decreased its radiance a fraction. As his sword fell from his hand, it faded away altogether. I tripped over the stairs behind me and we fell into a heap once more.

There was a sudden, startling silence. When I looked up, the angel had resumed its less fearsome aspect: strangely, it now looked like a gigantic, golden and muscular version of Anton, right down to the pencil moustache and the spats. Occasional curls of flame licked off it and finally died away entirely.

With a sudden burst, almost too fast to see, it picked up the matchbox from the floor and lifted it up in its enormous hand. The air came alive with a tremendous hissing of serpents. I trembled.

With one quick motion, the angel crushed the box into nothingness.

A small sound attracted its attention. Its head turned sharply towards the noise and ours followed. Over by the far wall, heading for the east transept door, we saw Barney trying to sneak away yet again. He let out a terrified squeal when he saw he'd been spotted and scrabbled at the door handle, finally getting it to work before slipping out into the night.

The angel dropped smoking ashes from its hand, and turned in pursuit, moving noiselessly. In its wake, the grimoire burst into flame on the flagstones and was soon reduced to nothing.

We were left alone in a stone universe.

'I hope he gives that rat-bastard what he deserves.' I let my head sink back onto the cold stone floor. Distantly, I could hear the sound of rain falling.

'"*As you plant, so shall you harvest*", Mr Dolan,' said a far-off voice, '"*your destiny is recorded on your forehead.*"'

I opened my eyes. Intricate lines of honey-coloured sandstone columns filled my vision, fading into the darkness above. A turbaned and bearded smiling face loomed over me.

'More wisdom from your holy book, Tegbir?'

He nodded and extended a hand to help me up. I accepted gratefully.

We stood there in the gloom for a moment gathering what energies we had left to us. Anton was all-in, pale and clammy, blood running from his nostrils, his clothes wringing with sweat; if we hadn't been there to prop him up, he would have collapsed back onto the floor like a rag doll. Tegbir gave me his sword to serve as a walking-stick and lifted his boss bodily off his feet, hefting him in his arms. I took the bent cigarette from out of my mouth and tossed it into the darkness.

Anton smirked at me from beneath heavy-lidded eyes. 'Not particularly respectful, Patrick,' he smiled.

'So, I'll say a few Hail Marys,' I replied. 'Let's get the Hell out of here.'

V.

"SKETCHED IN SHADOW"

SKETCHED IN SHADOW

"...UP OUT OF EREBUS THEY CAME, FLOCKING TO-WARD ME NOW, THE GHOSTS OF THE DEAD AND GONE: BRIDES AND UNWED YOUTHS AND OLD MEN WHO HAD SUFFERED MUCH AND GIRLS WITH THEIR TENDER HEARTS FRESHLY SCARRED BY SORROW AND GREAT ARMIES OF BATTLE DEAD, STABBED BY BRONZE SPEARS, MEN OF WAR STILL WRAPPED IN BLOODY ARMOUR—THOUSANDS SWARMING AROUND THE TRENCH FROM EVERY SIDE..."

- THE ODYSSEY - BOOK 11, HOMER (ROBERT FAGELS, TRANS.)

One thing I really hate is that sense, when you suddenly come awake, that you've been snoring. You don't hear it exactly—more like the echo of it and you look around quickly to see if anyone else has noticed. Looking around on this occasion, I saw a ring of annoyed elderly types, glaring at me, tight-lipped, in the gloom.

Sitting next to me, Anton coughed politely. 'Please excuse my friend,' he murmured. 'He's been working quite late hours this week.'

I straightened up in my chair with a muttered apology, hoping to God that I hadn't drooled down my chin. I couldn't really check on that without letting go of Anton's hand, or that of the old biddy on the other side of me, so I resorted to wiping my mouth on my shoulder instead.

We were seated at an oval table set into the bay window of a ground floor front parlour in a stately home in Sydney's inner west. The blinds had been drawn to dim the light and heavy drapes muffled the passing street traffic. What it didn't dispel, however, was the heat of the summer's afternoon coming in from outside and steaming the furniture polish off the gleaming table: sitting in close proximity to eight other people in this small nook, I was feeling stuffy and soporific.

'Let us continue.' The fellow in charge of this little gathering, stretched his shoulders and tipped his head back once more before closing his eyes. He was pale and dressed in a dark, bottle-green suit with a scarlet cravat. Like Anton, his hair was long, reaching down to the bottom edge of his collar, and swept back. He wore little *pince-nez* spectacles with a light gold chain trailing off one side of them down into his waistcoat pocket, the weight of which made them sit a little rakishly on the bridge of his nose.

'We call upon those departed to come and confer with us,' he intoned dramatically.

'Yes, please!' squeaked the old lady on my right, *sotto voce*.

'If there is anyone out there who wishes to speak, please give us a sign,' the medium continued.

Rather unexpectedly, a small tambourine on a side table behind Anton gave a little shiver, throwing a *frisson* of excitement into the gathering. Several of the ladies present gave sudden gasps of delicious surprise and stared around the table with eyes wide in the gloom. The exception was the dark-eyed medium's assistant in her turban and veils who preened a little and gave a knowing smile.

'We await your sign that you wish to speak,' the medium continued. I was about to observe that the tambourine had been a pretty clear indicator, but Anton squeezed my hand and gave his head a short shake.

'I would have thought the tambourine would have been sufficient,' the old girl gripping my paw leaned into me and offered in a stage whisper.

At that point a loud hammering boomed through the building, causing several of the ladies present to emit shrill, stifled screams. A balding fellow sitting around to the right of us, with a moustache that comprised the bulk of his personality, coughed and carefully reclaimed his hands.

'That's the front door,' he explained, before nodding and leaving to answer it.

'I didn't know ghosts used doors,' said my hand-holder, 'so polite!'

The medium uttered a short exclamation of annoyance and turned dramatically in his seat, resting his chin on his fist. His assistant leaned across and gently smoothed his shoulder. The moustache returned, borne aloft by its human pedestal.

'I'm sorry,' it quavered, 'but there's a messenger here for Mr Vadász.'

The medium threw his hands up in the air and turned his back on the table. Anton tapped my wrist with his finger to get my attention and jerked his chin towards the door. I prised my hand free from its deceptively steely captor and stood up, stepping away from the table with a few nods of my head to the gathered company.

'Sorry, have to go,' I said, 'duty calls.'

In the entrance hall, we reclaimed our hats and other bits and pieces and headed for the door, nodding to the moustache as we left. Out front, standing next to Anton's Oldsmobile which was pulled up to the kerb, was a well-padded, jovial-looking fellow, in a pin-striped russet brown suit and a white fedora. He flashed a hundred-dollar smile at us from beneath a pencil-thin lip fairy and squinted at us in the sunlight.

'Sorry to interrupt your meeting,' he said, 'my name's Armstrong, Clancy Armstrong. You're Anton Vadász, right?'

Anton threw him a frosty glare but acknowledged the statement with a nod.

'I figured,' he said, "recognised your car, with the elephant-headed fellow on the bonnet...'

'How may we assist you, Mr Armstrong?' Anton's voice was about to chill the afternoon heat.

Armstrong patted his jacket and then fumbled in an interior pocket. Pulling forth his visiting-card he said, 'I work in estate management. I have a young client who's experiencing some difficulties of a unique nature...'

'Spit it out Armstrong,' I growled, popping a match on my thumbnail, 'we're gettin' old over here...'

He stopped, looking at us one after the other while gracing us with his radiant smile.

'How would you like to investigate a haunted house?' he said.

* * *

We arranged a meeting a day later at Anton's Potts Point abode. I entertained the two fellows in the parlour while Anton gathered materials from his office and Tegbir poured drinks. Armstrong rattled on with a steady stream of monologue, knocking on the walls and test-driving the doors, during which his client stayed aloof, leaning on the frame of the French windows and nursing a cigarette while staring north towards the Harbour. A stiff breeze from that quarter had sliced away the humidity and the sunlight through the frangipani trees cast cooling shadows on the tiled veranda, but the young man—by name of Cyril Turner—seemed wrapped up in his own thoughts and careless of his surroundings.

He was a slight cove, muffled in a modern, dove-grey suit in the "Oxford bags" style, with a waspish face eternally settled into a frown of annoyance, like he'd just discovered he'd stepped in something unpleasant. He smoked elaborately, with a lot of attention to detail, like it was a magic trick that he was trying to perfect. When Tegbir presented a tray of cocktails to him, he took one, turned his pomaded head and sauntered across to an armchair in the far corner beneath a potted palm to get outside of it. If I'd had to sum him up in one word, I'd say "sniffy" about covered it.

Meantime, Armstrong carried on like a pork chop, wittering away at ten to the dozen about land prices and property sales, stuff that held as much relevance, or interest, for me as the last-placed horse in the Caulfield Cup. Still, I was content to let him colour the air for a bit, just nodding and throwing in the odd "ah!", and "I see!", until such time as Anton was ready for us.

He emerged from the library bearing an armful of books, which he placed neatly in a row atop the long table in the middle of the room. Then he turned and invited us all to sit down at the same, a request which Turner refused with a languid gesture of his hand. Instead, he puffed at his cork-tipped smoke and glowered out the window. Anton darted a glance at me; I just rolled my eyes and shook my head.

'St. Augustine,' Anton began, placing a hand upon the nearest leather tome, 'was quite categorical in his rejection of the spectral. He felt that ghosts could not possibly exist and rather, felt that any encounters with them must be misunderstood manifestations of the Divine will. That, or the wilful ignorance—or fabrication—of human agencies.'

Armstrong shot a quizzical look from Anton to me and back. 'Not this time,' he said, shaking his head. 'This is all on the up-and-up. We have ghosts to get shot of.'

'And that makes us—what? The local ghost exterminators?' I asked.

Armstrong's eyes went wide as he shrugged. 'If you like,' he said, 'I just heard that you two could take care of something like this—'

'I'm interested, Mr Armstrong,' Anton cut in, 'how *did* you come to hear of us?'

'The local priest,' Armstrong nodded, sitting forward to tap the tabletop with his finger, 'Reverend Denison, out at Windsor; he told me he couldn't do anything to help us, but he did give me your name, kind of on the sly...'

'This Denison a Catholic?' I asked.

'No—Anglican,' Anton answered before Armstrong could start rabbiting again.

'You know him then?' the estate agent asked.

'No,' Anton replied, 'the availability of clerical assistance across the City is something I simply like to keep at my fingertips. St. Augustine aside,' he continued, 'other figures within the early Church held vastly different opinions.' He reached forward to place a hand on the next leather volume.

'Pope Gregory the Great felt that the dead *do* communicate with the living, insofar at least as they could inform their friends and relatives of the conditions which they were experiencing in Hell, and to ask that masses and other indulgences could be sung for them in order to ease their suffering. He was of the opinion that the dead could manifest themselves directly to those whom they felt could best help them, or at least appear in their dreams.'

'I like this Pope Gregory fellow,' said Armstrong, 'he seems to have the stuff that we want.'

'I merely bring these two points of opinion to the table in order to delineate the field of play before us,' Anton explained. 'Our endeavour must encompass a wide range of possibilities from crude imposture to the acts of supernatural beings so we must be prepared for every contingency. We must cover the terrain as minutely as possible in order to ascertain the expression of the phenomenon, the better to attack its root cause.'

'And that's where I can help,' broke in Armstrong sitting forward, 'I can tell you everything that's been going on out at the property—'

'And I thank you for your willingness to contribute, Mr Armstrong,' Anton raised a hand, 'but this will require an outside perspective and fresh eyes. After all, the medium himself may be fooled into thinking that a tambourine has moved on its own, unaware that the device is being manipulated by his assistant through the agency of a black thread.'

'I *knew* it!' I exclaimed, 'I knew she was up to no good!' I downed the dregs of my drink.

Anton passed on to a third book, on the front cover of which he steepled his fingers.

'Both St. Augustine and Pope Gregory—along with many other commentators within the early Christian Church—were building upon a body of lore established by the Greeks and the Romans, notions of what the dead are, what they can do, how they behave. Homer describes them rather forcefully in *The Odyssey* as ferocious and terrifying, a hungry throng to be resisted with all one's might. Other contemporary writers codify the reasons for which the dead interfere with the living, ascribing motive and rationale—these range from the easily-solved need to find and bury the spectre's original body with appropriate rites, to the need to conclude unfinished, or thwarted, earthly business.'

'This all seems somewhat beside the point.' Turner piped up from the far corner; his words were couched in an affected *ennui*, but there was an undertone of anger seething just out of sight. 'I rather thought that you chaps would have some kind of, I don't know, a spray...?'

Armstrong coughed and leant in again. 'I mean, holy water? Isn't that the stuff? You just spritz it about a little and—*poof!*—no more spooks?'

Anton waved a dismissive hand and resumed his seat. 'Things of this nature are rarely that simple. If they were, your Father Denison would have effected the cure you suggest without hesitation. Instead, he referred you to us. Why? Because the Anglican Church has long since disavowed the so-called "Catholic Rite", the Rite of Exorcism, something which this situation—I presume, given his actions—very much calls for, in his opinion. It wouldn't be seemly of him to hand you over to a Catholic agency, so instead, he does the next best thing and gives you our details. However, even a killer of rats, Mr Armstrong, must ascertain the extent of the infestation and its means of access and distribution before providing a cure; to that end we must be allowed to conduct an appropriate investigation.'

Armstrong looked over at Turner who waved a languid hand. Anton's gimlet-gaze drilled the young man for a moment before he turned back to the estate agent.

'Now,' he said, 'can you give us the background to these events?'

Armstrong rested his hands on the tabletop and bent his head in conspiratorially. 'It's like this,' he said, 'I oversee the lease on a property owned by Mr Turner out west near Windsor. It's a decent spread—dairy farm—quite profitable, with strong connexions to the local community. Anyway, we're not sure of the details, but the previous tenants left—turned out the farmer was a dissipated, drunken sort of fellow. Since then, every time I get a new tenant installed, they leave shortly after, claiming spooky activity. It's happened twice now, and the place has begun to gain a reputation.'

'As haunted?' I asked.

'Yes,' Armstrong continued, tapping at the tabletop with his fingertips. 'And once a tag like that gets pasted on, it becomes more and more difficult to strip it off. You can drop the rent, but people want to know why; you can try and sell it quick and buyers get suspicious. Like I said, it's a very profitable business.'

'What is the form in which these hauntings take place?' asked Anton. 'You seem to be somewhat vague on the details...'

Over in the corner, Turner rose sharply to his feet.

'*Form*? What *form*?' he said tersely, all trace of affect gone from his speech. 'It's just—*haunted*. God, I can't believe I'm actually saying it! Whatever it is, it needs to be dealt with. Now, can you two take care of it as quickly, quietly and as cheaply as possible, or not?'

There was a momentary silence filled only by the sound of my jaw grinding. Anton regarded the lad coolly while Armstrong had the good grace to look a little embarrassed.

'Certainly.' Anton beamed at Turner, standing and circling the table to shake his hand. He placed his other hand on the lad's shoulder and proceeded to walk him slowly to the front door where Tegbir waited with hats and coats at the ready. Armstrong and I followed in their wake.

'Mr Turner,' Anton was saying as we joined them, 'have no fear that we will get to the heart of this situation in as effective and discreet a fashion as we are able to conjure. As to cost, we accept your task happily, whilst waiving our fee—rest assured that the intellectual challenge of the exercise will be reward enough.'

The look of surprise and delight on Turner's face could have lit up a lighthouse beacon. He nodded and shook Anton's hand once again before stepping out into the street.

'Say, that's mighty bully of you, sir,' Armstrong took his turn dangling off Anton's arm, 'I'll send over a spare key and the address tomorrow. I'm certainly glad I took the reverend's advice and tracked you two fellers down!' He plopped his natty fedora on his head and breezed out after his client. We watched them depart.

'You buying any of this, Anton?' I asked.

'Not a bit,' he replied. 'Let's try and work out what's *really* going on...'

* * *

The thing you notice first about Windsor is that it's flat. Not that Sydney is built on particularly mountainous terrain but, closer to the seaside, there's at least some degree of up-and-down. When you hit Windsor, the thing that strikes you is the complete absence of that. The second item you spot is the colour: it's very green out there. Flat and green beneath a huge blue sky. We spent a day getting there, following the Hawkesbury River back in from the coast, and found rooms at the Bell Inn on Little Church Street by late afternoon.

The town was homey and quaint after the grey drab of the Big Smoke. In the afternoon light, the little cluster of honey-coloured sandstone buildings at one end of the bridge exuded genteel country charm and represented probably everything that Lachlan Macquarie was aiming for when he set the place up. There was a light breeze building as Anton and I left the inn to take a turn about the neighbourhood, and a warm golden light was rolling over the Blue Mountains in the west to bathe the town in its glow.

'Not really the sort of place you'd come to looking for ghosts,' I said, lighting up a smoke.

Anton scanned the small community from the near end of the bridge, taking in the elegant church steeple, the stately poplars and the rest of the Georgian architecture.

'I think,' he said, 'that it's in just such places where ghosts make their most indelible impact. It's likely that—amid all the bustle of the City—we pass ghosts all the time and simply don't notice their presence. Here, the bucolic landscape throws them into sharp relief.'

I ashed my cigarette and jerked my chin towards a distant, truncated steeple. 'That Denison's church over there d'you reckon?'

'St. Matthews, yes. We should head over to the rectory first thing tomorrow and talk with him.'

'You think he'll have anything useful to say about all this?'

'Yes, I believe so,' Anton nodded. 'If not for him, we'd not be here. Anglicans don't formally acknowledge things like ghosts and exorcisms—or rather, they're not particularly forthcoming about them. More St. Augustine; less Pope Gregory.'

'As opposed to us Catholics, right?'

He nodded again. 'Denison could have steered Armstrong to the nearest Catholic church for a blessing and sanctification...'

'A little spritz of holy water?'

'Precisely. However, that would have exacted a toll upon his credibility, a loss of face as our friend Ji Daoyi might say. So, *we* get notified instead.'

'Lucky us,' I muttered.

'Indeed. And yet Denison could have brushed Armstrong off with some trite homilies, more in keeping with his church's view on such matters. Obviously, Patrick, there is something going on here that the Reverend Denison—at least—considers a threat.'

'And—speaking of Armstrong—what's your view of him?'

'I'm not sure—he's not really my area of expertise. He seems affable; open, even. Even so, I can't help but think that he's—how do you put it? "A little bit dodgy"?'

I snorted. 'He's a little bit dodgy in the same way that a lobster is a little bit hard to swallow whole. I did some checking up on him—put in a few telephone calls. There're no gaol-able offences in his background, but there's more than enough that seems a little shady if you take the time to look twice. We shouldn't really be surprised: you know what they say about estate agents—they eat their own young.'

Anton nodded, leaning on the bridge's handrail. I went on:

'What did you think of young Master Turner?'

'There, I think we have an issue, which is why I decided to disconnect with him financially. There is no longer a formal contractual basis between us—we have simply been invited to inspect a property on his behalf—and this, I think, will help free us up from some unpleasantness in the future. What did *you* think of him?'

'I think that someone needs to plant their boot in his arse and that, should I be the one called upon to do that, I will conduct myself with gusto. 'Can't stand uppity types. I checked him out too, with some old associates—it seems that Master Turner has racked up some gambling debts and, given his high-toned lifestyle, his inheritance is taking a beating. He needs new, cash-paying tenants out here, or a quick sale, to set things back in square. Otherwise, he's in deep trouble.'

'Yes, I thought there was something.'

The light had faded from the sky as we spoke and the first few stars began to ignite in the dark blue overhead. The breeze had developed a chillier edge, so we turned our steps back towards our lodgings. As I was about to toss my smoke, I caught some movement out of the corner of my eye and turned to look at the far end of the bridge.

'Is there a problem?' Anton asked.

I flicked my cigarette out into the dark towards the water rolling by below.

'Nah,' I decided, ''thought I saw someone over there on the other side. Probably just a shadow.'

The night closed in on us from all sides as we made our way back to the inn.

* * *

The next day, after a magnificent breakfast provided by our hostess, we sauntered the handful of blocks to the Anglican Church of St. Matthew and made our way around to the rectory. We handed our cards to the woman who answered the door and were invited to wait upon the Reverend's convenience. We were shown into a study and offered chairs. The room was small and a little shabby, neat but not obsessively so, with an impressive view across the cemetery towards the church.

Reverend Denison soon entered, shrugging into his black jacket in order to get down to business after having been—I supposed—disturbed at his breakfast: a strong whiff of toast followed along in his wake. He was tall and clean-shaven with short silver hair. He had the air of a gratefully retired military man, as though he'd gone to war unwillingly, out of a sense of duty, and had returned after acquitting himself satisfactorily to put all of that behind him. He held both of our cards which he scanned as he sank into his desk chair: I assume he'd read mine first and thought nothing of it; when he clocked Anton's though, he froze slightly and frowned before sitting down.

He took off his steel-rimmed glasses and shot each of us a quick appraising look. 'I assume that Armstrong sent you?' he said.

Anton dismissed the notion with a wave. 'Mr Armstrong has contacted us, yes,' he said smoothly, 'but we are not in his employ. Neither are we working for his principle.'

Denison tapped our cards on his blotter before dropping them into a small tray to his right. 'So why have you come?' he said.

Anton sat forward, steepling his fingers in front of him. 'They told us some interesting things concerning a local property,' he said, 'however, it is those things of which they did *not* speak which have piqued my interest. There are lines Reverend Denison, and there is the reading of what lies between them. I'm aware of why Mr Armstrong wishes us to be here; I'd like to know why *you* do.'

Denison sat back in his seat and fired guilty looks at the both of us. He fiddled with a fountain pen while collecting his thoughts and then said:

'You're right. This is a bad business. There's something strange going on over at the Middleton's dairy—it's not something that I can, officially, get involved with—but there are other circumstances at play here too—flesh and blood, every-day things—which are all wrapped up in it. My sense is that you can't get at the one without broaching the other and being thus intertwined, no single agency can take it on board. Did Armstrong tell you the circumstances?'

Anton shook his head as he sat back again. 'He was prepared to be most forthcoming,' he said, 'but I decided to await the opportunity of a less vested interest.'

Denison nodded and rolled the heavy pen away. 'And you think my version will be any less so?' he said.

'That's as may be,' responded Anton, 'at least you and I will be—what is the expression?—"playing on the same wicket"?'

Denison chewed on that for a bit then sat forward gripping his hands together before him on the desktop.

'What would you like to know?' he asked.

Anton waved airily. 'Everything,' he said. 'From the beginning.'

Denison turned his head to look out across the lichen-scabbed headstones, then sat back and looked us both in the eyes.

'I hope neither of you have anywhere urgent to be,' he said, 'because this will take a while...'

***

'The first I heard about the situation,' began Denison, 'was when I was called to the pub—the Macquarie Arms—to answer an emergency. I had just finished writing my sermon for the following Sunday so, when the call came, I was ready to jump in. A boy from the hotel was standing by the front door in a state of excitement—you know how young lads can get with things like this—and Mrs Geoffreys was interpreting for him, telling me that there'd been murder done down at the 'Arms and that I was needed.

'I headed off as quickly as I could. We're not a large community and I know everybody who lives here: I was making a short list of likely suspects in my head as I entered the pub—running the various feuds and disagreements of a number of local hot-heads through my mind for likely victims—but when I saw who it was, you could've knocked me over with a single breath. The last person I expected to see lying there was Percy Middleton.

'As it happened, he wasn't actually inside the hotel. He was lying in the stable yard out back, just at the gate entrance that leads out onto the road leading to his place. He'd been knifed a few times in the back—he was unconscious when I arrived and dead soon after that. I gave him the Last Rites straight away; even Dr Morrison who arrived some moments afterwards, said that nothing more could've been done for him.

'Percy Middleton was the last person anyone 'round here would want to murder. He was hard-working, a good husband and father; he liked people and people liked him. He took care of his business and, I believe, things were going well for him in that regard. He was always available to lend a hand: a few years ago, during the floods we had here, there were a couple of outlying farms that went underwater and Percy wouldn't rest until those families had been sheltered at his place and until he'd worked himself to the bone helping to round up their stranded and bogged livestock. That's the sort of fellow he was—he knew that such things could just as easily happen to him.

'I hadn't seen him to talk to in the days before the murder, but he seemed in high spirits—happy as Larry; at ease...

'Of course, my immediate duty was to his family. I set out straightaway to the farm to see what I could do for Margaret, his wife—now widow—and their child. When I got there, she was in shock, hysterical, wanting to see her husband immediately. Word gets around in small towns, and it wasn't surprising to me that she'd been told everything before I got there. I made arrangements with the other women who'd gathered there, to look after the child and the house, and I helped Mar-

garet up into the buggy. We trundled back into town, she gripping my arm the whole way, wide-eyed like she was desperate
to believe that some kind of mistake had been made.

'Of course, there was no mistake. She viewed the body at
the doctor's surgery, and it pulled the stuffing right out of her.
Mrs Geoffreys and I brought her back here and put her to bed
to sleep things off. We found her before dawn the next day,
wandering about the house, wondering where she was and
how she could get word to Percy that the cows needed milking.
Morrison came by and gave her a sedative to calm her down.

'Of course, there was an inquest. Those of us who'd been
involved gave our evidence and it seemed that it would be
all cut-and-dried: murder by person, or persons, unknown. I
learned that Percy had gone to the bar late in the morning
and had ordered a beer, unusually for him at that time of day.
Let me be clear—the man was no saint, but this wasn't his
normal behaviour. The barkeep said that he was in high spirits, very pleased with himself and in a mood to celebrate. He
spoke to some friends and even placed some money on a horse
race through the SP bookie and won—not a huge amount, but
nothing to sneeze at either. All in all, he'd been having a great
time and left soon after midday, not drunk according to the
barman, and intending to head home.

'We were all questioned as to whether we'd seen evidence
of his winnings during our examinations of the body, but none
of us had. It was presumed that his good fortune had also been
the motive for his demise.

'With all the sordid back-and-forth of the inquiry I was surprised to see Armstrong there, taking a keen interest. I hadn't
seen him at the hotel during the incident, so I wasn't sure how
the affair could concern him. I put it down to the fact that

these things can be a strange source of fascination for any-body. I was soon to learn otherwise...

'A couple of days later, Margaret came to the rectory and asked to have a word. I put aside whatever it was I was working on, and immediately made myself available. She had become pale and drawn, a shadow of the woman she'd been. She sat here in the office and asked me if I'd seen Percy's satchel when I'd tended to him—a leather bag with a long strap that he used to carry cash and documents. I hadn't noticed any-thing of the sort, of course, and I said so. She nodded and then stood up to leave. I made some comment along the lines that, if Percy's winnings were in such a bag, then it had most likely been taken by the murderer. She just nodded and left. Later, I found out that she'd asked Dr Morrison the same question.

'Well, life began to fall back into its usual round. I'd asked Mrs Geoffreys to keep a weather-eye out on the situation and one day, she appeared at my office door and asked me to fol-low her. She led me to the front parlour and held aside the net curtain of the window that looks out onto the street: through it, I could see Margaret sitting on the kerbside across the way, rocking her child in her arms and with a suitcase by her side.

'Straightaway, I went out and picked her up, leading her into the Rectory and sitting her down. Once we had stowed her things and Mrs Geoffreys had taken care of the infant, I asked Margaret what was happening. She was vague and distracted; withdrawn. She seemed unwilling to speak, and what little she said was couched in the most bitter terms and cadences. She had been evicted, she said. Percy had gone to the land agents on the day of his death to make the final payment on their farm mortgage. The agent said that he'd never made it that far, implying that the temptation of a drink and a flutter on the horses had waylaid him. They had no record of the payment on their books. Margaret told me that she was sure that Percy wouldn't have gone astray, that the last payment was something he'd been keenly looking forward to: she was sure that the payment had in fact been made but, without a receipt or any other document to prove it, it was her word against the agency's. The owner had thus resumed possession of the farm and she'd been evicted with little notice.

'Of course, I was outraged. I told Margaret to stay for as long as was necessary at the Rectory and I took my anger around to the land agent's office. I was referred to Clancy Armstrong who told me that it was all out of his hands—no payment had been made, no record of such a payment had been entered, no receipts issued to that effect. What could he do? He was a slave to the demands of the property's owner and he'd been instructed to find new tenants as quickly as possible. No appeal to his sense of charity had any effect—it was like talking to a smooth and shiny stone. I left in disgust and went to the lawyers who look after matters for the parish and asked them what could be done.

'As it turned out, they couldn't do much. Without documents saying that the final payment had been made, nothing could be proven; the owner and his agent were well within their legal—if not moral—rights. I helped to find Margaret a position here in town and, at her own insistence, she found a place to live. She took the child off to her mother's place where it could be looked after in safety and then returned, despite my saying that perhaps a new situation would be better for her as well. She absolutely refused to leave: she is convinced that the receipt for her husband's monies is still here somewhere and she has been doggedly following every lead to its resolution. So far, there has been no sign.

'That would probably have been the end of things; however, it all changed when the new tenants moved in.

'The first ones to take up residence were a father and son who'd moved to the area from up in the Hunter Valley. They kept pretty much to themselves—I guess it was something to do with being new to the region and unsure of what kind of reception they'd receive—I believe they'd been coached a little by Armstrong to expect a stiff resistance from the locals. I did my duty, went out to talk with them and welcomed them to the neighbourhood. They didn't really talk much—I don't believe a single word passed between myself and the father; the son was the more forthcoming, but I wouldn't exactly call him garrulous! My visit was strained and I'm not sure which of us was the more relieved when it was all over.

'Imagine my surprise then, some nights later, when I was awakened by a pounding at my door. There were the new tenants, in their sleeping attire. The father was all but carrying his son who was bleeding down his face from a savage head wound. I urged them inside, and we tried to mop up as much of the blood as we could. I sent Mrs Geoffreys to fetch Dr Morrison and they soon came back to stitch up the poor lad's head.

'Tight-lipped as he was at our first meeting, now I could barely keep the older man from talking. He raved on about rocks being thrown in at them from outside the house, stones floating past them through the air—even passing straight through the roof! He said that he and his son had been awakened by banging on the walls and that his bedclothes had caught fire without reason. As they fled the premises, they spied an old brick hovering in front of the house, quite six feet off the ground. The son had tried to grab it and it had pitched itself at him, catching him on the forehead. It was all quite fantastic, the things he told me, but here they were; and here was his son, injured and unconscious.

'I consulted with Morrison afterwards, after he had given both men a sedative to ease their sleep. He said that he'd heard of such things but had never given them much credence. He suggested that we both visit the farm and investigate for ourselves.

'We did just that the next day. We went all over the place looking for signs of the disturbances that the older man had mentioned. We found scorched bed linen in one of the bedrooms which seemed to confirm his story but, standing on a chair next to the bed was a beer bottle, a pouch of tobacco, a pipe and a box of matches, which—taken altogether—painted a more down-to-earth picture. We visited the neighbours and arranged for them to look after the farm's beasts while the new tenants stayed in town and they were quite willing to help.

'A few days later, the two men left. They gave no indication that they were going to do so; they just grabbed everything and ran off under the cover of night. I wrote several letters to the Hunter region—Singleton, specifically—using what scraps I'd eked out of them to try and pin down where they'd come from and where they'd likely go back to, but nothing came of it. I also had a visit from Armstrong, puzzled about the disappearance and curious as to what part I'd played in it. I assured him that I'd heard no more or less than Morrison—he'd spoken to him also—and he soon left, saying that, while he was down a tenant, they'd paid their first quarter's rent up front, so he was still ahead.

'Then came the Wilsons. They were a young family, escaping the City where they'd made a meal of things, trying and failing to run a small grocery business there. They'd washed up—after paying off creditors—just about even, with enough money borrowed from family to afford rent on the farm. They were open and friendly, although frankly, I thought, a little bit naïve with regards to the lifestyle that lay ahead of them. I spoke with them at length and they seemed sure that the milk that they could produce and sell in their first month or so would more than cover the rent and other sundries accrued during their first quarter of residency. I wished them luck but resolved to keep a watchful eye on them.

'Less than two weeks later, I was again woken up in the night by a commotion at my door. This time it was the two Wilson children: they were terrified, claiming that their mother was being murdered. I left them in Mrs Geoffrey's capable hands and sped out to the farm to see what was happening.

'When I got there, I could see Wilson hammering on the front door of the house, yelling and screaming for all he was worth. When I approached him, he pointed his rifle at me—I came pretty close to being shot, I can tell you! He was wild—pale as a sheet and covered with blood from wounds to his face and body. He told me that Mrs Wilson was locked inside, and he couldn't get in to save her (this was winter, you'll recall, and they'd put up all the shutters before retiring). I offered to help and—when I turned the doorknob—the door swung wide, easy as you like. He was bewildered, claiming that he'd been pounding on it with all his strength and hadn't been able to budge it. I believed him—if only because of the state of his hands and the blood he'd left on the woodwork.

'We went inside, and it was cold. I don't mean cold for a winter's night, but *deathly* cold; unnaturally so. We walked to the main bedroom and...'

The Reverend stopped suddenly. His brow wrinkled and he swallowed a few times, suddenly uncomfortable in his dog collar. He shot a glance at me and fiddled with his fountain pen some more.

'I have not,' he picked up the thread once more, 'spoken of this to anyone. I saw it; Wilson can vouch for it because he was with me and he saw it too. The whole time, I couldn't believe what I was seeing. I felt like I was going mad. But for the fact that Wilson was in a worse state than I and needed my help, I feel I might well have lost my grip on reality entirely.

'Mrs Wilson was floating over the bed. *Floating!* She hung there above the covers, closer to the ceiling than the mattress, her eyes open but unseeing. And she was blue from cold, gentlemen, almost frozen. Wilson yelled and ran over to help her but, as he got close, I heard a loud growl—awful it was—and he was hit, suddenly, by something I couldn't see. He just dropped to the floorboards and lay there, completely insensible.

'I'll confess I've never felt so scared. I said a short prayer and crept slowly over to the bed. I was on tenterhooks: I expected at any moment to get the same treatment that Wilson had, but nothing happened. I reached out my hand to touch Mrs Wilson and, the moment I touched her arm, she dropped to the mattress, bouncing heavily on the springs. Instantly, a loud pounding noise came out of the walls, adding to my fright: I grabbed her off the bed and dragged her from the house, then ran back to do the same for her husband. Fortunately, he had begun to wake up and we both managed to get us all into my buggy and on the road back into town. But there was one more fright in store for me that night:

'As we ran away, I turned back to look at the farmhouse once more and—and gentlemen, I swear to you that this is absolutely true—hanging by itself in the air above the footpath to the front gate, was a single brick; I could see it as clearly as I see you now. And while I watched, it just dropped onto the ground, like someone had let it go.'

There was a moment's silence after he'd finished. He pushed the pen with a sense of finality to one side and then sat up in his chair, rubbing his face briskly with his hands. He seemed unwilling to meet our gazes and contented himself with making sure that nothing on his blotter had gone astray while he had been talking.

'Make whatever you want of that last bit, gentlemen—ignore it; give it credence—whatever you want. I'm prepared to make statements for whomever you ask, if that's of any use.'

Anton shot me a sidelong glance then leant forward in his seat.

'My thanks, Reverend Denison, for so candid and detailed a report,' he said, 'rest assured that we have no need of proofs to verify your story—we have experienced much in our careers and we can tell when a speaker has met with the kinds of things that we have. There is no requirement that you repeat your account to any third party, and we will not be making a report of any kind, or any notes, other than those which will facilitate our investigation while we are here.'

He nodded and looked mightily relieved.

'What did Armstrong have to say about the Wilsons?' I chipped in. I figured I'd warmed a seat long enough.

Denison snorted. 'Well, he said he was concerned and that he hoped things would be resolved. Of course, he was tied up in red tape, he said; he had a client whose interests he was duty-bound to serve, *and* the lease was legally binding...' He waved his hand.

'So, of course, he couldn't see his way clear to helping the kids out of their situation by waiving the deal and handing back their rent money,' I finished for him. 'What a rat!'

'Exactly,' said Denison, 'he claimed to feel pity for them, but he wasn't prepared to help—it was all out of his hands. I managed to get Wilson taken on as a farmhand at one of the neighbouring properties. The congregation set up a collection to raise money for train tickets to send his wife and their children to live with her parents in the Blue Mountains while he earned enough to dig them out of the hole they'd gotten themselves into, but Armstrong? He didn't lift a finger.' Denison punctuated this last sentence with several digs at his blotter with his own digit.

Anton leant forward sharply then stood up, languidly stretching, like a cat.

'I am deeply appreciative of your time, Reverend,' he said, 'and, now that we have a more complete—and reliable—version of the events that have taken place, I feel that the time has come for us to take action. Patrick! Let us go and make use of that key with which Mr Armstrong has so thoughtfully provided us.'

* * *

The day was fairly advanced about its business by the time we stepped out onto the street once more and headed back to the centre of town. We orientated ourselves and split up: while I sussed out the scene of the crime, Anton ducked into a small grocery store a short step down from the turn off to the road leading to the bridge.

Our road out of town to the dairy farm ran east past the Macquarie Arms Hotel, a dusty road that wound its way over the gently rolling landscape. I stopped to light a cigarette by the open gate that let into the stable yard behind the pub and reflected that it was a pretty ordinary place to meet one's end, face down in the dirt and the horse apples. There were a few outbuildings bordering the yard but no real fence to speak of—anyone wanting to sneak up on a lone walker and do him a mischief had every opportunity to do so. While engaged in these thoughts, Anton caught up with me carrying a large brown paper bag and indicating that we should be getting on.

We sauntered on towards the edge of town following the road and the wall of poplars that formed a windbreak along one side of it. The sun was approaching its noontime maximum by that stage and beat down hard. Pale billows of dust flew from our footsteps and cicadas deafened us from the trees. I shrugged off my jacket and hooked it by a finger over my shoulder; I was interested to see if Anton—laden as he was—would do likewise before we got to the farm.

The road wound along in a slow arc, rising gently before cresting and heading down a slight incline. As we began to descend, we clapped eyes on the dairy farm at last. It was nestled within a stand of low greenery at the end of a straight dirt path that led from a gate in the fence running parallel with the road. The single-storey structure was bound on all sides by wide eaves projecting over an encircling veranda, throwing the house into deep shadow under the midday sun.

"Looks fairly ordinary,' I observed, dropping my smoke and crushing it with my shoe.

'Appearances aren't always as reliable as they ought to be,' Anton replied, mopping his brow with his handkerchief.

We stepped through the gate onto the path. There was a loop of wire that allowed the gate to be held open, so Anton secured it before proceeding. I shot him a quizzical look to which he responded by shrugging his shoulders. We crunched our way up to the front door. Under the wide eaves, the porch was covered with dead leaves. The front door bore signs of ill-use and ominous brown stains on the panel-work. The shutters were still in place, so I spent some time removing the one closest to the front door to allow a little light within. Reaching into my coat pocket, I handed Anton the key to the front lock. He put down his bag, clinking with bottles, and tried the key in the door. It turned after a little heaving and we were soon inside.

There wasn't much to the joint. A central corridor ran from the front door to the back and two rooms opened off this on either side. If there was a kitchen, it was most likely in one of the outhouses around the back. There was a small amount of well-worn furniture and an odd assortment of personal effects—a broken doll; a couple of pieces of cutlery; a tea tin; a crushed empty box for Ardath-brand cigarettes. The whole place was crying out for a good dust and airing.

Anton strode forward to the rear of the structure and began to fumble with the bolt on the back door. It swung open with a groan and he stepped out into the shadows of the back porch, the midday sun kicking up a huge glare beyond that startled the senses; a blue-tongue lizard that had been sun-bathing on the back steps, slithered off into a cranny in the woodwork with a dry rasp. Anton put down his paper bag and looked out into the back yard of the farmhouse, enclosed by three out-buildings and partly overshadowed by a spreading oak. He put his hands on his hips and nodded.

'This should do,' he said.

This was one of those times when I felt that Anton's planning had sped far ahead of my understanding, so I lit a smoke and sidled up to stand beside him.

'What's the plan, Anton?' I asked.

'We are going to dig a small pit in the centre of this yard,' he said, gesturing with his hand, 'about the length and depth of a forearm—a cubit as the old reckoning would have it. There should be a spade, or shovel of some kind, equal to the task in one of these buildings...'

'And by "we", I assume you mean "me",' I said, sticking my cigarette in my mouth and hanging my jacket on the corner of the fly-screen door behind us. Anton nodded and went on:

'Then we'll have to build a fire at one end of it—just a small one. No need to get carried away on a day like this.'

'Then what?' I said, rolling up my shirt sleeves.

He pulled a small notebook out of his waistcoat pocket. 'Then we summon the dead,' he said.

I stopped for a moment to let that sink in.

'"Summon the dead"?' I said at last. 'Isn't that more of a midnight kind of thing, rather than something you'd do in the middle of the day?'

Anton was striding across to a pile of firewood stacked against the side of the house under the eaves for easy access. 'Any of the cardinal times of the day should work equally as well,' he said over his shoulder, 'and I, for one, would prefer to try our luck in the daylight, rather than the dead of night.' He started selecting pieces of wood from the stack.

I shrugged and looked around. Selecting one of the out-buildings I went in search of a shovel...

We soon had what we needed, and I had laboured to produce the required pit—a cubit long and deep. The tinder caught quickly in the day's heat and we soon had a merry little fire going, its flames almost invisible in the white glare of day. Then Anton squatted down and started pulling objects from the paper bag he'd brought along. First was a bottle of sweet sherry which he handed to me, knowing I had pocket-knife with a corkscrew; the second item was a small pot of cream with a spring-loaded lid. Next, he reached out a paper parcel the top of which had been rolled down and tied shut with string. Then he pulled out a jar of honey and stopped, squinting into the near-empty bag. It has to be said that some ominous stains had begun to ooze through the stiff material.

'The rest can stay there for now,' he said.

By this time, the sun was well-and-truly straight overhead. Anton turned around, finding the best angle from which to begin and lifted his notebook to start.

'Wait, wait!' I said, interrupting, 'what do *I* do?'

'I'm going to start making the offerings,' he said, looking around piercingly, 'I'm not sure who's going to show up—someone will have answers to the questions we want to ask—and that person is who the offerings are for. Everyone else will have to stay back until we've gotten what we want. Get ready to keep the interlopers away from the presents.'

I pushed my hat down on my head and lifted my fists. 'So, it's gunna be a bunfight?' I asked.

'That's pretty much how Homer described it,' he said. He stood up and wiped sweat from his brow, shaking his hands at his sides then taking a deep breath. 'Let's begin,' he said.

He lifted his notebook again and began reading from it, something in another language. The tone of it was urgent and angry, rising and falling in cadence. At one point he stopped and reached down to lift the bottle of sherry: this, he poured out in a circle around the edges of the pit. Then he read some more. I stared to get a crawly feeling at the base of my neck—could've been sweat trickling down my collar but it felt like someone was watching us unseen. I turned around, this way and that, trying to make out where they might be. Anton stopped again and hefted the cream jar, pouring it out in a circle over the sherry; he tossed the empty jar to one side when he was finished. Then it was back to the reading.

He repeated this with the honey and then with handfuls of barley drawn from the small paper bag. The effort under the midday sun showed in his features—he was sweating heavily by the time he neared the end. That's when the first one tried to get past me.

I clocked him out of the corner of my eye. He sprang out from between the bakery and the tool shed, thinking he could slide by me while my back was turned. He was in his shirt-sleeves and braces, bearded and with his hat pulled down throwing his face entirely into shadow. I swung round to grab him and managed to get one hand on his shoulder. Strangely, my fingers seemed to sink right into him, letting me feel the bones within. I pulled, trying to throw him off balance and—disconcertingly—he flew up onto the roof of the house porch. I didn't have time to marvel about it though: across the way two more figures had broken cover and were throwing themselves at the mess Anton had made.

The sheer numbers of them had me working hard to try and keep them at bay. In my favour, they seemed to be composed of something light and flimsy, so one good punch would send them flying, a good shake would quiver them into nothingness. They darted like swallows through the sunshine, using its glare to mask their approach, their features all rendered blank by the shadows of their hat brims. They made weird high-pitched squeals, like bats or mice, and they were terribly, *terribly* cold to the touch.

'How much more of this, Anton?' I yelled, shaking my hand to combat the numbing sensation of frost.

'We're almost there!' he answered. He bent down and hefted the stained brown-paper bag. 'You! There in the back! Stand forth!'

He indicated a figure hidden in the shadow of the oak tree. It shuffled a little uncertainly, then stepped forward into the streaming hot sunshine. In most respects it was like the others of its kind, who hissed and withdrew at its approach; however, this one was jacketed and hatless, its bald pate vanishing in the harsh light of the day. Its eyes were sunken, mired in darkness and strings of spittle swung from its lips to tangle horribly in its beard. In certain angles of the light, its skull was clearly visible through its flesh.

Anton stepped forward holding up his hand to prevent further approach. 'What was your name?' he ordered. The shrilling of the cicadas pulsed in the surrounding gum trees and rang across the searing hot day. I wiped sweat from my eyes, turning constantly to watch the other dead men lurking like a flock of currawongs all seeking their chance at a piece of carrion.

The black-jacketed figure worked its jaw a few times as if out of practise. Eventually, thin words issued forth, as if from a considerable depth.

'Thomas... Turner...' it hissed between rictussed teeth.

Anton and I exchanged confused glances.

'You know Cyril Turner?' I asked.

The figure took a step forward suddenly and waved an angry arm at me, making me lift my fists once more.

'Don't!' spat the ghost, lanyards of spit twisting through the air. 'Wastrel! Layabout! Don't say his name!'

'Then he is... your grandson?' ventured Anton.

'No kin of mine!' the angry hissing continued, 'disowned him, I did! 'Meant to cut him off, but... too late! Too late!' The ghost grabbed its head with both hands and tore violently at its flesh. Around him, the other sun-bleached figures crept forward slightly, but Turner's shade fell into a crouch, baring its teeth at them and growling bestially—deep, guttural and feral. I felt a chill slide down my back despite the heat.

'All this!' the old man's shade turned to us once more, 'I built all of this! And now he pulls it apart! Throws it away! It's gone, all gone. Gone...' His thin voice trailed off.

'What has he done?' Anton asked.

The old man's cavernous eyes looked up at him; a cold light shone briefly in their depths.

'Something terrible,' he whispered through spittle-slaked teeth, 'a terrible deed, done to an innocent man...'

Anton stared at the phantom for a bit, then upended the paper bag, spilling its contents into the pit. Two freshly killed rabbits thumped heavily into the dust. The old man was on them in a heartbeat; a horrible rending sound reached our ears. In its wake, the other ghosts moved forward but Anton and I stepped in their way, driving them back until the old man had finished. Eventually, they retreated into the bushes and the black, devouring shadows.

When they'd vanished, we turned around to see how the old man had gotten on, but he had disappeared too—nothing was left of the rabbits except some bones and sinew, with a few blowflies picking over the remnants. Anton gestured, and I started shovelling the dirt back into the hole, trying to hold on to my breakfast.

While I was patting the earth back down flat, I said: 'Well, that was horrible. D'you get what you wanted?'

Anton, dusty and sweaty and covered in soot, was rolling his sleeves back down. 'Certainly not what I expected,' he said, 'but I think we're forwarder along.'

* * *

We didn't go straight back to our digs. Anton headed to the post office in order to send a telegram, while I found a barbershop that sold cigarettes.

'Packet of Red Capstans?' I asked the pomaded fellow pushing a broom. He nodded and moved off to the shop counter.

'You're lucky,' he said, 'I'm almost out—won't see another delivery until early next week.'

'I'll smoke 'em slow,' I lied, 'whaddaya got if I run out?'

'Just some pouches of shag and papers,' he said glancing across the stock, 'unless you like them cork filters?'

I made a face. 'Not my cuppa tea,' I said, 'you get much call for fancy smokes out here?'

'Nah,' he replied, 'we get this young feller, comes here occasionally from the City. He smokes 'em so I got a carton of Ardath in to keep 'im happy. They'll probably go stale before he gets through 'em though.'

I turned to go, lighting up, and then stopped, squinting back at him through the smoke. 'Ardath, huh? 'Blonde kid? 'Face like a smacked arse?'

'That's the chap,' smiled the shopkeep, 'you know 'im?'

'Wish I didn't,' I said. I touched the brim of my hat and stepped outside. Anton, looking dusty and uncharacteristically dishevelled, walked over to me.

'All set?' I asked him.

He nodded. 'If Armstrong's in town, I expect we'll hear from him in an hour or so.' He looked at his watch. 'Otherwise, I guess he'll contact us early on the morrow. I need to change.'

We headed off to the Bell Inn, taking a circuit which wound past the Macquarie Arms Hotel to the bridge and then through the cooler air along the bank of the river.

'Say, Anton,' I said, stopping and grinding out my cigarette underfoot, 'd'you reckon we sent all of those ghost-blokes back to where they came from?'

'It's not an exact science,' he answered squinting up at me and running a finger around his collar, 'but that's how the procedure is supposed to work—we summon them and then send them back. Why do you ask?'

"Cause I thought I just saw one of 'em standing over there at the other end of the bridge.' I shaded my eyes with my hand and stared in the direction I'd indicated. The river sparkled in the afternoon sunlight and the road at the bridge's far end shimmered in a shifting haze.

'Nothin',' I said, shrugging, "just gettin' jumpy I s'pose.'

Anton let his gaze linger in the distance for a while longer, absently stroking his moustache. 'Perhaps,' he said at last; then: 'let's go—I need a bath.'

Flurries of dust in the rising breeze of the afternoon followed us home.

* * *

The next day, we rose early to another heaping country repast and then made our way to Reverend Denison's place. He invited us into the study once more and we spent some time in idle chit-chat. Soon, a distant bell rang, and Mrs Geoffreys pushed open the study door to announce a visitor.

'It's that Armstrong person,' she said, distaste dripping off each word.

Denison indicated that she should show him in, and he erupted into the small room, a ball of nervous energy, shaking hands and crushing his hat in his fist. Some of the grease had slid off him: he looked worried and his oily sheen suffered accordingly.

'Hello again!' he piped, 'all well? Good. Good. I hear you have something for me?'

We all started to resume our seats but, since Armstrong's presence left us one short, I offered him the one I'd been using and sauntered over to the window.

'I take it the train journey was a pleasant one?' Anton asked Armstrong casually.

'Yes, yes,' he replied, looking for somewhere to put his hat, 'all good.'

'You know, we should really have thought to come by train, Patrick,' he said to me. I waved a hand in acknowledgement.

Armstrong looked from one of us the other and back, his hand tapping manically on the armrest.

'The carriages are really quite congenial...' Anton continued.

'Will you forget about the damned train?!' Armstrong burst out. In the frosty silence that followed, he at least had the good grace to look ashamed.

'I-I mean to say,' he stammered, 'don't we have business to be getting on with?'

'Do we?' Anton leaned forward, smiling like a dealer with his hooks in a needy snowdropper.

Armstrong gaped at him, then scrabbled in his coat pocket.

'You sent this telegram,' he stated, unfolding it on his knee '"*Talked to the ghosts; all is revealed*". What do you mean—"*revealed*"?'

'Excuse me,' I said standing up from leaning against the window-frame, 'I'll be back in a tick.'

'I mean to say,' he went on as I opened the study door and stepped out, 'if there's something going on at the farm, as the agent, I should be told—'

I closed the door on his weaselling and turned to Mrs Geoffreys, waiting in the front entrance hall.

'Could I bother you to show me the rear exit, Mrs G.?' I smiled.

Out in the back yard of the Rectory, I hopped the side fence, sped around to the main street and crossed to the other side. Then I walked slowly towards the church, angling for the cemetery just alongside it. A figure, in worn clothes and a dusty hat, was leaning against the graveyard fence, trying to act casual, but also trying to see in through the Reverend's study window. I crept up behind him and whispered in his ear:

'You're looking a bit rough, Cyril. What, is it laundry day?'

He shrieked and jumped like I'd poked him with a hatpin. His face flushed in the aftermath of his shock and he wheeled away from me, trying to escape, his features settling once more into their habitual expression of angry resentment. I grabbed his shoulder and he slapped me away, trying to shield his face with his hand.

'C'mon, Cyril,' I cajoled, 'I can see that it's you.'

Still, he tried to pretend he wasn't there, so I let him try, poking at him and grabbing his costume, steering him where I wanted him to go. Finally, he screamed angrily at me, a breathy exclamation, seething and frustrated, like an effete growl, and took off towards the centre of town. I lit a smoke and watched his progress, following in his wake.

After trying to lose me in the intervening streets, he ran along the side the Macquarie Arms and ducked into the stable yard through the side gate. I jogged along the street, past the pub's front entrance and peered around the corner towards the backyard on the other side. As I watched, Cyril emerged, sneaking past the outbuildings in a manner suggesting long familiarity and dodging a trailing growth of blackberry. Once clear, he scurried off towards the bridge. I put on some speed, caught up with him once more when he was about a third of the way across and kicked his feet out from underneath him. He hit the planking with a heavy thud.

'Steady on, Cyril,' I said, 'you've come all this way and you got dressed up 'specially. Don't you *wanna* have a chin wag?'

By way of answer, he did the breathy-growly thing at me again and tried to slide away from in front of me, his palms slapping and scraping on the deck, shoes scrabbling for purchase. I stomped on his instep to stop him getting too far along.

'Y'know, Cyril,' I said, 'I can *see* you. I *know* who you are, and you know who *I* am: it's no use pretending otherwise. You can't just give me the cut direct and think this isn't happening, because—you know what?—it is. This isn't George Street; it's Windsor—different rules apply.'

He was gasping and seething, trying to push my foot off his while angry tears ran down his face. I made sure he couldn't get away.

'Why so desperate Cyril?' I asked, taking a drag on my smoke, 'you got a car parked over there some—'

I stopped. In the clear morning sunlight, the bridge road shimmered brightly, little mirages wobbling across its surface. At the far end, I saw what appeared to be a man standing there. He was in his shirtsleeves with dark trousers and a waistcoat, and with a full beard. His hat was pulled down low, its crown bled white by the sunlight and its brim shadowing his face in darkness. The thumb of one hand was hitched in his trouser pocket; the other lifted up on an extended arm and pointed to the south, over the side of the bridge, towards the far bank. As I watched, the figure melted away into the blue light of the day.

I snapped out of it in time to see Cyril win free and get back on his feet. He tripped and stumbled a bit, arms flailing and managed to get a few steps forward before falling on his face again, his backside poking up towards me.

I pulled my smoke from my lips and murmured, 'With gusto.' Then, I kicked him as hard as I possibly could.

* * *

Quite a bit later, we were sitting in Anton's parlour, musing after one of Tegbir's sumptuous meals. Through the northern windows the sky was blood red as the sun descended and a light breeze stirred the frangipani trees, filling the room with a light, sweet perfume. I sniffed my brandy and listened to the faint sounds of traffic outside.

'How was the trial?' I asked, 'I noticed they didn't call *me* to give evidence.'

Anton stretched in his chair and shrugged. 'It was fairly straightforward,' he said. 'There was enough physical and circumstantial evidence to place before the judge with which to convict Young Turner on the charge of murder. It would not have served anyone any good to mention ghosts or any supernatural activity—it would simply have gotten in the way of the due process.'

I cocked my head at him.

'But there *was* supernatural activity,' I said, 'we both saw what we saw.'

'Of course,' Anton put his brandy down carefully on a coaster, 'however, to quote St. Augustine, it was all "sketched in shadow on certain images of things that are real". You had already found all the evidence that was necessary to lead to a conviction—the cigarette packet in the farmhouse; the missing satchel containing the receipts for Middleton's mortgage payment along with the knife used to kill him...'

'...Which his *ghost* pointed out to me, buried on the riverbank at the far end of the bridge,' I interjected.

Anton waved his hand. '*How* you found it is of no relevance to the legal proceedings; that you *did* was all that mattered.'

I grunted, shrugging down into my chair, my legs stretched out in front of me. 'Sometimes it feels like all this going one-on-one with the spooks and demons—and angels, let's not forget them!—is all for nothin' if no-one else gets to hear about it.'

Anton chuckled. 'Fear not Patrick,' he said, his eyes twinkling, 'I keep meticulous journals of all of our cases, and this one not least. Someone someday will read all about our exploits. You might even feel tempted to write of them yourself.'

I scoffed, then sniffed. 'I would've loved to've been there when they sentenced Armstrong,' I said smiling grimly, 'that reptile is right where he deserves to be...'

'Amen to that,' said Anton, picking up his glass once more and lofting it in a toast. We sat in silence for a bit.

'You know,' said Anton, 'our work doesn't go entirely unrecognised. Reverend Denison is aware of our efforts. And Margaret Middleton—now rightful owner of her husband's farm—is grateful for our efforts on behalf of her family. To these few at least, we are the heroes of the day.'

'"Heroes", huh?' I chuckled softly, 'I can drink to that.'

We clinked crystal in the ruby dusk.

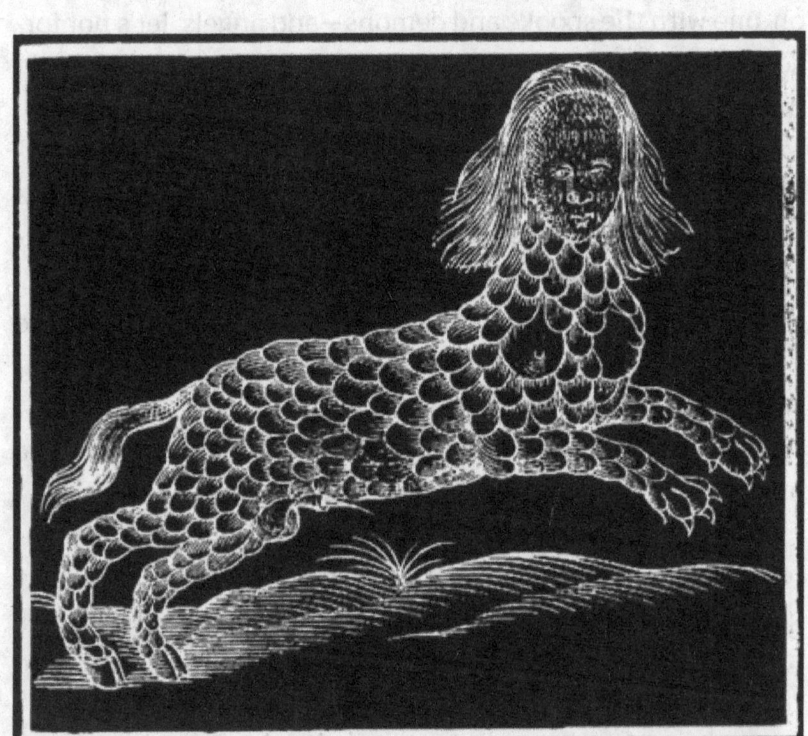

VI.

"A GORDIAN SHAPE"

A GORDIAN SHAPE

"...HER HAND IS A NET, HER EMBRACE IS DEATH; SHE IS CRUEL, RAGING, ANGRY, PREDATORY; A RUNNER, A THIEF IS THE DAUGHTER OF HEAVEN..."

- MESOPOTAMIAN INCANTATION

I popped a match on my thumbnail. Lighting my smoke with its yellow glare, I flicked it into the gutter next to the car tyre where it sizzled into lifelessness. I leaned on the Oldsmobile's hood and craned my neck upwards: high above me the bump of drums and a skirl of clarinets wafted down from the lit windows of an upper storey—the *Fifty-Fifty Club* was in full swing. High clouds shot grey by a brilliant full moon swept by overhead in a bruised sky: but for that one slice of light, the Chard Building on the corner of William and Forbes streets, was a dark silhouette.

I turned around and leant on the car's roof, eyeing the shadowy streets around me—my watch told me it was quarter to midnight. Archie was running late. Which was ironic because, two days ago, if you'd asked me, I would've told you confidently that Archie had been shot in Gaza during the War and was, indeed, the late Archibald Poole.

There was a rustling in the darkness across the street, which I put down to the business of rats. I looked at my watch again and decided to give Archie ten minutes more of my life...

A side door behind a phalanx of tin rubbish cans cracked open and wan golden light washed out into the alley. The thin shrieks of rodents announced their annoyance at being interrupted. I flicked away my smoke and squinted into the dark.

Archie materialised shortly thereafter. He was short—as jockeys are meant to be—and dressed in the bellhop livery of the *Fifty-Fifty*, tight-fitting, parti-coloured red–and-black with plenty of gold buttons and a silly pillbox cap turned to a jolly tilt. I noticed that he kept playing with the chin strap, walking it forwards and backwards with his stubble. His hair was lank, black and greasy and his eyes jaded; I'm pretty sure that the moustache was not especially *de rigeur*.

'You're running late, Archie,' I complained, 'I was just about to stand you up.'

'Sorry,' he winced, 'it's jumping up there tonight; tricky getting away.'

'Cigarette?' I offered.

'Ta,' he replied, quirking a smile and taking the Red Capstan in his grey-gloved fingers.

We blew smoke for a bit.

'I heard you caught a bullet at Beersheba, Archie. What happened?'

He shrugged. 'Didn't take,' he said. 'I spent a lot of time in hospital afterwards though. Months an' months. 'Caught the slow boat back home.'

'And now working here instead of back at Randwick?'

He leant his back against the side of the Oldsmobile and shuddered, crossing his arms.

''Couldn't do it,' he said, 'I've had enough of screaming horses to last me a lifetime...'

'And so, you've thrown your lot in with Phil Jeffs and the *Fifty-Fifty*?'

'The job was going,' he shrugged again, 'and I fit the monkey-suit...'

We smoked a bit longer in silence. Archie was just as I remembered him from our racecourse days when he was the big-time jockey and I was a star-struck kid hanging around the stables, eager to please. Now however, he was world-weary; a little dissolute; at odds with the hand Life had dealt him.

'What's the story, Archie,' I broke the silence, 'why have you brought me here?'

He sighed and ashed his cigarette on the footpath. Then he tipped his head back to look up at the lights, marshalling his thoughts.

'A few months back,' he said, 'there was a raid. Nothin' unusual: the jacks on the payroll kept most of the straight coppers downstairs and the search was pretty much a lick-and-a-promise, as arranged. But there was this new kid, bell-hop like me; didn't know the drill; panicked. He said something about not wanting to go to gaol and ran away. Anyway, a floor below the *Club*, he tripped on the stairs, flew down the last set and broke his neck.'

'Ouch,' I winced.

'Yep,' Archie drew in some more smoke, 'it was pretty messy, but handled in the usual way—bit of cash here and there, Bob's your uncle...'

'And now...?' I prodded.

He dropped his butt to the concrete and ground it out with the tip of a highly polished, be-spatted shoe.

'Now he's back,' he said.

'"Back"? As in... his ghost?'

Archie nodded. 'We see him all over the place: lurking in corners; hiding in the dark—even out on the main floor with the customers. It's hard to spot him: we all look the same in these outfits with the lights down low...'

I bounced my cigarette off the side of the building.

'Alright, I can work with that,' I said, 'I know a few tricks...'

'...It's the kitchen staff, mainly,' he went on, 'Antonio, the head chef, almost blew his stack; threatened to quit. One of the kitchenhands claims that it came at him with a knife...'

'Archie,' I interrupted the flow of details, 'don't worry about it: it's just a ghost. I can deal with it. Show me where it happened.'

We entered the building by the same door Archie had used as an exit: he kicked the half-brick out of the road to let it close all the way behind us. There were a lot of stairs: wooden-balustraded marble risers in switchbacks from landing-to-landing between the floors, like Jacob's Ladder leading to—I dunno—the opposite of heaven. I was panting by the time we'd cleared half of them.

'You're losing a bit of form, mate,' Archie noted, waiting for me at the top of the next set of steps, 'this soft life's doing you no good.' The way he said it was odd: not joking or pointed, just an observational tone, without humour. Like he was summing-up a horse before race day.

'I've still got it where it counts, Archie,' I responded, 'don't you worry about that.'

'Up here's where it happened,' he said jerking his chin towards the next set of risers. The mad scurry of jazz wafted down from above, tinny in the poisonous yellow light of the stairwell.

I joined him at the bottom of the next set of stairs; he was standing pointedly against the wall rather than in the centre of the landing.

'He tripped about halfway up those steps,' he said with a gesture, 'and this is where he ended up.' The grey-clad finger described an eloquent and terminal arc.

'Good a place as any to start,' I said.

I dove into my coat pocket and pulled out a small octagonal piece of painted wood with a tassel hanging off one end. From the other pocket I produced a small cobbler's hammer and a couple of tacks.

'What's that?' Archie asked nervously.

'Chinese mirror,' I answered, 'it has a funny name I can't pronounce but it keeps spooks away. I'm gunna nail it up here at the end of the stairs...'

'Alright.' He looked a bit apprehensive about all this—maybe he was worried about me ruining the woodwork. 'I have to be getting back,' he said, 'can I leave you to it? When you're done, head up the next flight of steps and use the door marked "kitchen"—I'll let them know to expect you.'

He scampered away like the ghost had suddenly appeared next to me.

Shaking my head, I got down to business. I nailed the mirror up high where it might not be noticed and might be out of reach if it was. Then I lit a cigarette followed by a trio of joss-sticks and I burnt a handful of Hell-money: there were a bunch of words that my friend Daoyi usually mumbled while all of this was going on but I chose to utter the spirit of the incantation in English, in *lieu* of the letter:

'Hey sonny-Jim: you've had your fun, now take the smoke and the cash and bugger off.'

Then I packed up my stuff and lumbered up the next flight of stairs, flicking a few drops of holy oil about me as I passed…

The kitchen was in full swing as I entered, with the sound of ringing knives and barked commands; the smell of searing beef set my stomach rumbling. As I stepped through the door, I almost ran into a young kid in white with a blue stripe-y apron: the moment he clocked me he turned as pale as the plucked chook he was carrying and went weak at the knees.

'Hey mate,' I said quickly, grabbing him by the shoulder, 'I ain't no ghost. Can you tell me where Antonio is?'

Amid all the noise and flaring gas jets, I managed to wrangle the staff together for a makeshift exorcism and benediction. In the midst of it, the floor manager burst in to demand why the flow of eats to the *clientele* outside had stopped but I glared at him and told him in certain terms to buzz off. He took the hint. When it was over, I shook hands with a grateful Antonio and his minions all cheered around us.

I decided that my work was over and now, having never experienced the delights of the *Fifty-Fifty Club*, I wanted to see what all the fuss was about.

The four-piece band was about halfway through a loud and creditable version of *"It Don't Mean A Thing If It Ain't Got That*

Swing" as I pushed through the kitchen doors into the heat of the main floor. I snaffled a glass of champagne from the loaded tray of a passing bellhop and savoured the contents as I viewed the surroundings. The band members were all in tuxedoes and lit from below with dim golden light, giving them the appearance of frenetic demons; couples, hidden in shadow, stumbled about the central dance floor, under the eddies of smoke stirred up by the ceiling fan, embarked upon various approximations of the foxtrot, or the Charleston; dim lighting at the tables revealed tinted glasses of sparkling liquor—along with cigars and small bowls of cocaine—and glittered off the jewels of those seated about them. All around the perimeter of the space, the windows were standing open, letting the heat and noise of the gathered occupants out into the dark. With all the music and the yelled conversations, I could barely hear myself think.

While I watched, the dancers parted momentarily, and I caught a glimpse of a slight figure moving purposefully along the far wall. I immediately recognised his gait and—what with the long hair and the sturdy cane—I knew that this was my colleague, Anton Vadász. What the Hell is he doing here, I thought. I dropped my glass onto another passing tray and struck off across the parquet floor, dodging the jigging couples.

By the time I made it across, he was nowhere to be seen. I craned my neck trying to look over the heads of the crowd to catch a glimpse of him through the drifting haze but to no avail. Suddenly, a whistle blew, sharp and discordant against the pumping jazz, and the lights went up, causing everyone to blink in the sudden radiance. Someone grabbed me by the elbow and spun me around.

'It's a raid,' said Archie in my ear, 'let me get you settled so you can ride it out.'

He steered me towards a far corner where the lighting was less intense. There, a small table stood against an open window with four chairs, although only one of them was occupied. Archie pulled out an empty seat and dropped me smartly into it. With a deft movement, he picked up the champagne bottle, produced the end of a strong cord attached to the wall from behind the nearby curtain and, using this, dangled the bottle outside the window by its neck. The champagne glass he tossed carelessly out into the night. Then he pulled a pack of cards from a pocket and began dealing them across the cocaine sprinkled tablecloth.

'There's only two of you,' he said, as three-quarters of the jazz ensemble high-tailed it to the kitchen and the pianist broke into something slow, complex and classical, 'so, what? *"Gin rummy"*?'

'Are you serious?' I said.

'*"Go Fish"* it is then.' The pasteboards flashed expertly into place.

'Right,' he said, standing up again, 'now, as you recall, this is the *King's Bridge Club* and you're simply waiting for the opportunity to make up a foursome. Don't say anything else to the nice policemen which might cause them any alarm.' With a quick nod, he was gone.

I shot a glance across the table to its other occupant. Her long fingers scooped up the cards and she quickly fanned them appropriately. Her bobbed hair was black and smooth with deep blue highlights, like it had been lacquered. Her skin was china-pale with stark crimson lips and her eyes gazed hotly at me, two bright pinpoints of light in a veil of kohl like a smoky haze. She wore a dark sable coat over a glittering, shimmering dress of golden beadwork and a white egret feather curled upwards from the golden *bandeau* over her sleek bob. Her movements were slow and sinuous, veiled by the black fur that hung carelessly, exposing one pearlescent shoulder.

'Do you have an ace of hearts?' she breathed. I felt the short hairs at the back of my neck stand on end.

I stared blankly at the playing cards lying in front of me, then snatched my fedora off my head.

'Um, my name's Patrick,' I said, 'Patrick Dolan. In case anyone asks us…'

She smirked a wry smile and extended a be-ringed hand across the table towards me. I took it in my paw, and we shook hands, although it felt like I ought to have been kissing her delicate fingers instead.

'Call me Amalia,' she said.

'Amalia,' I echoed, 'that's—'

'Well, look who knows a thing or two about *"Bridge"*,' a harsh voice broke in. 'And here I thought you'd have trouble getting your thick head around *"Snap"*, Dolan'.

I looked up sideways. Standing next to the table with his hands on his hips was "Kangaroo" Jack Campbell, a local detective known as much for his turn of speed as his doggedness in tracing thugs to their lairs. He squinted down at me, his jaw thrust forward, clenching a smoke between his thin lips.

'Actually, Detective Campbell,' I said, 'it's *"Go Fish"*. The lady and I are just waiting until a table becomes available…'

'Stow it, Dolan. I thought you were supposed to be some kinda professional spook-hunter nowadays. Where's your offsider?'

I feigned nonchalance. 'Oh... around here somewhere.' I folded my cards together and stood up. 'You're absolutely right Campbell—we investigate strange events. I'm here to try and stop a haunting on the premises and the lady was just helping me with my investigation...'

Campbell stepped closer, looking up at me with his teeth bared.

'You're certainly up to *something*, Dolan, and I'll get to the bottom of it eventually, you *and* your partner. For now, I've got other fish to fry. You and your lady-friend stay here and keep out of my way. Are we clear?'

I lowered my head so that we were practically nose-to-nose.

'As cut glass... Detective,' I growled.

He touched his hat-brim briefly to the lady at the table and turned on his heel to get back to business. Across the room, a handful of outraged people were being led away by police officers, while the floor manager tried to reason with whoever seemed to be in charge. Campbell gave him short shrift.

'My, that was exciting.'

I turned my attention back to my partner in pretend cards as a shiver flittered over me. She was sitting back in her chair firing her smoky gaze up at me with her head tilted sideways. Her coat had slid a few inches more off her shoulder revealing the thin strap of her dress and the shadowplay of curves formed by her collarbones beneath it. A steady pulse beat at the side of her long neck. I gulped and sat back down quickly.

'Sorry about that,' I said, 'Campbell's all talk. He and I go way back.'

'You're a... policeman, too?' she asked, sitting forwards.

'No; not even,' I said with a laugh, 'we just grew up in the same part of Town.'

She regarded me with her glittering stare and trailed her fingertips across the tablecloth, her painted nails snagging in its tired weave; I noted that they were long and lacquered a deep, almost-black, green.

'He said that you have a partner with you here tonight.' Her voice expressed petulance. 'Which one is she?'

'"She"? You've got the wrong end of the stick, there. Anton's not a "she", and I just *thought* I saw him here; I'm not even sure it *was* him...'

She sat up quickly and leaned forward over the table, moving close, close enough so I could see that her eyes were emerald green with golden flecks. Her perfume coiled in the air between us.

'Then you are here alone, too?' she smiled through pointed teeth. I could do nothing but drink her in and nod dumbly. My heartbeat rang in my ears.

'Excellent,' she cooed, 'and here I thought that this night was wasted...'

After the jacks left the party, the festivities began again in earnest. As the lights quickly dimmed, I hauled the bottle of champers back inside through the window and poured drinks for the two of us. We clinked glass and settled in for some murmured conversation while the music switched from Bach back to Bix Beiderbecke.

'Tell me, what does a "spook-hunter" do?' Amalia asked, reaching across the table to smooth my tie.

'Well, we—that is, my mate Anton and I—we look for ghosts and such; the odd demon occasionally; and we get rid of them...'

'"Get rid of"? You mean—*kill*?'

'Sometimes,' I admitted; 'some of these beasties are pretty evil...'

She leaned in close, her elbows on the table, her eyes narrowing.

'Surely, you can't judge a creature for simply being true to its nature?' she asked. 'After all, you wouldn't destroy every lion on the planet for hunting and eating gazelles?'

'I dunno about that,' I said, 'ghosts set out to cause harm; demons do evil because that's what they are—pure evil. Even angels aren't all they're cracked up to be.'

'You would destroy an angel?' She used a finger to turn my head in her direction. I swam deep in her golden gaze.

'Well, sure,' I chuckled, 'if it was on a rampage and innocent people were in trouble...'

She sat back in her chair and I felt her fingernails trail away, scratching off my chin.

'You hold innocence in high regard,' she pouted.

I shuffled my hat on the tabletop, aligning it in the corner of the wooden surface alongside my smokes and lighter.

'I really don't bother too much with that end of things,' I said, 'Anton is the one who keeps track of all those right-and-wrong questions—I generally just punch stuff.'

She leaned forward again and ran a hand from my shoulder down to the centre of my chest, causing me to momentarily stop breathing.

'And I'll bet you do that very well indeed...' she cooed. The top of my head felt like it was going to float away.

She sat up briskly and snatched my cigarettes off the table. 'Tell me,' she said lighting up, 'what are you two working on at the moment? An interesting pursuit?'

I pulled a cigarette out of the packet that she handed to me and she lit it with my lighter after igniting her own.

'It's a bit of a dead-end,' I said, putting the smokes back to one side. 'Anton caught the whiff of what he thinks is some kind of vampire. Not much to go on—people going missing; usually at night; all in a run-down area around an alley near here, off William Street.'

'Its lair…?' she prompted.

'Something like that,' I nodded. 'We found an old derelict house. The street level was just a shell after being burnt out in a fire, but there was a basement that had remained largely intact—that's where we went.'

'And you found…?'

I breathed twin streams of smoke out of my nose. 'Nada. Nothing. If anything had been holed up there, it was long gone. We were back to square one.'

'"Square one"?' She raised an eyebrow at me.

'Y'know, *"Snakes and Ladders"*? The kid's game? You keep trying to move forward, but you step on a snake and get sent back to the beginning? They didn't play that where you're from?'

She fanned smoke away with her hand and stared out through the window into the dark. 'I had a very sheltered upbringing,' she said.

'I'll bet,' I said.

She snapped a piercing look at me. 'Why do you say that?' she said.

'Don't take this the wrong way,' I placated, 'but you obviously have money—you need five pounds just to get *out* of this joint, never mind what they charge to let you in. *Or* what they're asking for this hooch.' I twirled the champagne in my glass. 'And the way you're dressed? You've got more class than any of the other sheilas here. And yet you're sitting alone.'

She sniffed. 'Why shouldn't I sit by myself?'

'You're alone because you don't know anyone in this crowd. I'll bet you were just bored and lonely and decided to come see if this place lived up to its reputation.'

A hint of colour mounted her cheekbones and she ducked her head to draw quickly on her cigarette.

'I see you're very observant, Mr Dolan,' she said.

'I'm a private investigator,' I said, 'it's what they pay me for. Don't get cranky...'

'Do you like to dance?' She stood up quickly, sloughing-off the sable like an old skin, and stretching luxuriantly.

'D-dance...?' I quavered.

'Yes,' she replied, 'I may have come here alone, but now I have a partner. Come.'

She dragged me out onto the floor and the struggling couples already there parted before us. I was hesitant: my skills in dancing are just about equal to waltzing with my Aunt Beryl at a Saint Pat's Day shindig, but hardly more than that; Amalia could throw more choreography into breathing than I'd seen most people capable of. I wasn't sure what kind of paces she'd put me through; I resolved to just try and keep up.

As it was, I don't think my feet touched the floor. She let me lead and then she twirled around me like a wisp of flame, subtly moving me where she wanted us to go and making me look good while she did it. Her dress flashed and dazzled, and her delighted smile thrilled me in a way I'd never felt before. When a slow tune kicked in, I held her close and she felt like magic. Probably the black kind.

'Isn't that your friend over there?' She broke into my reverie, her lips so close to mine that I could feel her breath on my face.

'Hmm?' I said, woozily.

'Over there,' she spun away from me waving her hand at a point to one side of the dance floor.

I circled around her bringing her back into my arms and looked to where she'd indicated: at a table, hidden by the gloom and the drifting smoke, sat Anton, in a red, pin-striped suit, carousing with a bunch of other fellows. He was puffing away on a huge cigar and laughing with a group of shadowy individuals of whom I could only make out their flashing, pointed teeth and yellow cats' eyes. Lounging on the tabletop, Anton's elbow was firmly sunk in a plate of greasy chicken drumsticks and he sipped from a tumbler of something greeny-brown and smoky. The group of them seemed to be enjoying the spectacle that Amalia and I were presenting.

'He certainly seems to be enjoying himself,' Amalia observed.

'Yeah, he does...' I replied. I'd always known Anton to be more of a strait-laced kind of bloke: seeing him cutting loose as he was here left me feeling somewhat disconcerted, like something somewhere was deeply wrong. 'Let's sit the next song out...' I mumbled.

I steered Amalia back towards our table, and she retreated with some reluctance. As I pulled out her chair, she grabbed me by the lapels and spun me round, pushing me onto the seat instead. Then she plonked herself down in my lap, light as a feather and cool as limestone, and snuggled in close. The chair creaked alarmingly beneath us.

'Well, we seem to be getting along just fine,' Archie's voice cut through the smooch-induced haze in my head, 'more champagne?'

'Um, sure,' I murmured, gently pushing Amalia back and sitting up, trying to straighten my clobber. My mouth tasted sweetly metallic from her waxy lipstick. Archie poured and I snatched up the glass even before he could plonk the bottle down on the tabletop.

'Have fun,' he smiled with a mock salute and shimmered off into the dark.

Somewhere in the gloom, a woman shrieked in drunken laughter—it sounded like a horse screaming in fear. I put down my glass.

'Look, Amalia,' I said, 'I have to go see a man about a dog. I'll be back shortly, alright?'

She chose not to answer and, instead, lifted her glass and took a swig, eyeing me over the rim with her smoky gaze. Her silk-sheathed legs crossed slowly, and her dress shimmered intriguingly in the dark. I turned reluctantly, shuddering, and headed towards the kitchen.

I wasn't sure if it was the champers, or the heady after-effects of being kissed, but I staggered rather than walked across the main room, like the floor was swaying beneath my feet. At one point I toppled sideways into a table of patrons, smacking my hands down on top of it to break my fall.

'Hey! Beat it, buster!' A slick-haired fellow in a dark suit jerked his thumb towards the door to reinforce his message. I mumbled something apologetic as I stood upright and, I could have sworn that the lad sitting across from me was being operated on: the front of his shirt was sticky and red and the other customers sitting on either side of him were dipping into his torso with their fingers and an assortment of cutlery, laughing and chatting all the while.

'I said: *beat it!*' The dark-suited fellow stood up belligerently, causing me to back away.

'Yeah. Sorry...' I staggered backwards holding up my hands.

I turned to look at the dance floor: all the dancers were engaged in some kind of shimmy I'd never seen before, keeping low and circling the open space with their heads down. Some gimmick of the lighting had bursts of dull red luminescence streaming up the walls at sporadic intervals from the trendy fittings, in time to the louder jabs of the jazz tunes. For some reason I couldn't fathom, my flesh crawled, and my heart was lodged firmly in my mouth. Somewhere in the dark, that drunk woman laughed again.

'Dolan!'

I swung around trying to work out where the voice had come from. My head wasn't working straight, and my feet were somebody else's. A hand grabbed my arm and the connexion gave me something to anchor onto.

'This way, Dolan! You're exposed out here in No Man's Land!'

I blinked. There was a digger hanging onto me, full uniform from puttee'd boots to slouch hat and with a rifle and bayonet slung over his shoulder. A lank, greasy wing of hair flopped over his forehead from beneath his brim and his upper lip was adorned with a trim black moustache, like an inky thumb had wiped a dark stripe beneath his nose. On the wall behind him, in time with a heavy beat on the bass drum, a burst of red flame jetted upward from the light fitting.

'Archie...?' I said, as little fragments of rock and dirt pelted off the surroundings.

'Yep, it's me,' he said hauling me off the dancefloor. He pushed open the kitchen swing door and held it open with one foot while gesturing me inside. In the light that streamed from within, I noticed the hole in the front of his jacket and the red stain that had seeped out around it.

'Archie! You're shot!' I gasped. 'Are you alright?'

He glanced down at his chest dismissively. 'Yep,' he answered, 'it didn't take.'

He pushed me roughly through the door and we fell inside just as the stoves belched a cloud of fire. We both ducked and scurried across to the stairwell exit-doorway, keeping our heads low.

'Right,' Archie said leaning his back against the wall and pulling back the bolt of his rifle, 'this is as far as I can go. You need to get in there and go up, get out of this mess. Someone will meet you on the other side.'

I was trying to get all of this straight in my head. Nothing seemed to be making much sense.

'Why can't you come with me?' I asked.

He put his hand on the door and shook his head with a rueful smile. He walked the chinstrap of his hat back into place by stretching his chin. 'Some kinda booby-trap,' he said, 'I can't get past it, but you'll be alright.'

I shook my head to try and clear it of all the fuzz. 'How? And what happened to your monkey suit?'

He laughed. 'It's just a uniform, Dolan,' he said, 'one's very much like another.'

He pulled open the door and manoeuvred me through. 'Be a good boy Pat-o,' he said, 'and stay on track. Just like at the racecourse.'

A cloud of fire erupted from the ovens behind him as he pushed me through and slammed the door after.

In the stairwell all was dark and cold. I couldn't hear anything; not even the bump of the jazz being played inside the 'Club. All sense of community had vanished to be replaced with a strong sense of being watched, of something inimical lurking nearby. I turned slowly and my shoes squeaked on the floor. As I circled, a bright glint of light flashed into my eye. I recoiled from it, just as you do when a sharp reflection from afar strikes you and makes you move your head, trying to find the best position to avoid it. I raised my arms to shield myself.

The light was coming from the wall at the far lower end of the set of stairs leading back down to the street. Once I'd worked out where it came from, I soon saw that it was a beam of light from the octagonal mirror which I'd hung up there earlier on. I didn't know why it was shining like that—there didn't seem to be any other source of light striking it and being reflected—but slow cogwheels began to turn inside my brain.

The light shone up from below and threw an octagonal shape behind me on the wall of the landing on which I stood. I held up my hand in the bright radiance, seeing it turn bluey-pale, and then turned to face the next set of stairs heading upwards. Archie had said to go up—what had he meant by that? Was I supposed to go up to the roof?

'Patrick!' I looked up and saw a dark figure on the landing of the next floor above. The light dazzled my vision, but I could tell that, whoever it was, they were wearing the bellhop uniform of the *Fifty-Fifty Club*, stupid pillbox-hat and all. They gestured frantically.

'Patrick! This way! Quickly!'

'Alright, alright,' I growled, 'no need to yell...'

I stumbled forward and fell hard onto the balustrade. My feet kept tripping on the risers as I fought my way up the steps. For some reason my legs had turned to rubber and my hands felt like they were made of sodden wool. Still, I pushed forwards, climbing the handrail wrought ironwork like it was some kind of crazy sideways ladder and using my arms to drag my useless legs up from below.

Suddenly, gloved hands grabbed me by the shoulders and hauled as hard as they were able. I scrabbled with useless limbs trying to lend what aid I could, although it was probably more of a hindrance than a help. Other hands joined the first pair and I felt myself bumping upwards until I fell flat onto a hard, dusty surface. I was rolled quickly over onto my back.

Above me I saw crumbling walls on all sides; high beyond them was a misty sky with a bright full moon directly overhead, fading the nearby stars with its glow. A person leaned in, looking down at me: they were wearing the black-and-red livery of the *Fifty-Fifty* which wasn't so strange, given where I thought we were; what *was* weird was that it was Anton who was wearing it.

'That monkey suit really doesn't work for you, mate,' I said.

He reached forward quickly grabbing my neck with his gloved hand; I took the time to notice that there was some grizzled old bloke on the sidelines with a lantern and a scared look on his physog. I realised that Anton was checking my pulse and so I switched my gaze back to him. Suddenly, he wasn't wearing the ridiculous uniform anymore, just his regular clobber.

He reached into his vest pocket and pulled out a small glass ampoule which he proceeded to crack under my nose.

'Sorry, Patrick,' he said tersely, 'but we need to get out of here and you are simply too heavy for us to manage.'

Whatever was in that phial, it sent lightning into my brain and down my spine and got me up on my feet in two shakes. Anton and the old geezer propped me up from either side and we raced across a sooty, exposed stretch of floor, through some scorched, tumbledown masonry and out onto a street where the Oldsmobile was parked. As we drew near, I felt my legs starting to turn to jelly once more. Anton threw the rear door open and I fell prone onto the back seat. Minutes later, the engine fired up and we started rolling away. I let myself drift with the night...

* * *

Some weeks later, I was trying to have a shave in the digs that Anton had arranged for me. Shaving was tricky as I had to manoeuvre around all of the bite-marks on my face which were still trying to heal. I'd been told that they wouldn't be so noticeable given time, but for now any dreams I had about being a matinee idol had to be shelved.

I was in some kind of retreat run by the Greek Orthodox Church under the stewardship of Anton's friend, Father Miklos. The other tenants here were all priests, or monks of some kind, and any female presence was thin on the ground. The prevailing idiom was Greek which meant that I had no idea what anyone was saying around me, other than when Father Miklos had something important to impart. He was an affable so-and-so, permanently decked-out in a black robe with a funny hat, like an upside-down top-hat. He had a flowing white beard and his eyes twinkled behind an ancient set of spectacles. His voice was high-pitched and raspy and, in English, his esses were hard and sibilant, which occasionally caused me to flinch.

I had no idea how I got there. The last thing I remembered was that evening at the *Fifty-Fifty Club* which, I'd been informed, hadn't happened as far as I remembered it at all. I'd spent quite some time in bed, tossing between nightmares and panicked episodes in which a lot of Greek priests held me down while Father Miklos chanted steadily and flicked holy oil at me. Eventually, the fever broke, and I woke up in this white room with sunshine streaming in through a wide-open window. I was ravenous and, despite being unable to walk, I would have dragged myself anyplace that would give me something to eat...

It took some time before I was strong enough to stand, let alone walk, but soon I was on my feet once more and Tegbir dropped by with some clothes and other essentials that allowed me to start getting myself back together again.

I put the razor down on the edge of the sink just as a quiet tapping came from the outer door.

'It's open,' I said.

I stepped out into the main room to see Anton enter and close the door behind him.

'Well,' he said, giving me the once-over, 'you look much better.'

'I'll *feel* better,' I said, 'when my face isn't a bleeding jig-saw puzzle.'

Anton waved a hand. 'Give it time,' he said, 'things will improve on that score.'

I grunted and shrugged into my braces.

'I see that you're feeling stronger,' he observed, 'that's a good sign, anyway.'

'Standing up is half the battle,' I said, stuffing an arm into my jacket.

Anton regarded me with his head tilted slightly, tapping a gloved finger on the head of his cane.

'Do you feel up to a talk with Father Miklos?' he asked.

I picked my hat up off the back of the austere wooden chair on which it was hanging and straightened up, stretching my shoulders and feeling the deep lethargy that still wrestled with my system.

'Sure,' I said; 'he feelin' chatty?'

'He wants to talk about you going home,' Anton replied, 'and about making sure that something like this doesn't happen again.'

I stopped and stared at him, flexing my jaw. I could feel the scabs complain as I did so.

'I'd like to have that conversation,' I said evenly.

'Very well.' Anton swung the door wide and stepped aside to let me exit.

We walked along the slate tiles of a wide, white-washed corridor lined with many rooms, like the one I'd been installed in. Across from the doors to these cells were large windows with many-paned glass panels, thrown open to admit the mild air and the sunshine. The outside walls of the building were clad with clusters of orange and scarlet bougainvillea and tendrils of this gorgeous foliage trailed inside. As we moved along, a young priest scurried past, nodding his head at us as he did so.

'Friend of yours?' I asked Anton.

'No,' he responded, 'I believe he's your neighbour. You've given him quite a few sleepless nights.'

'Oh.' I turned to see where he had gone but saw only his back as he vanished around a far corner of the hallway.

After some turnings and a few stairs, we ended up in front of a serious-looking door on which Anton rapped with his cane. A voice called admittance, and soon, we were seated in Father Miklos's office in padded chairs across from where he reclined at his leather-topped desk. Behind him a broad window gave us a view of a lush garden surrounding a wide driveway beyond, with glimpses of other wings of the sprawling building. The office was cool and lined with bookshelves all stuffed with tomes labelled in Greek writing. Here and there on the walls, icons stared impassively down at us, gleaming softly golden.

'Well, you're looking much improved,' Father Miklos beamed at me his eyes shining behind his lenses. His voice was lightly accented and despite having a rough edge to it, had a surprising tenor lilt.

'Yes, thanks to you fellows,' I said.

He waved a dismissive hand and swung his chair sideways to stretch his legs. 'It was the least we could do,' he replied.

'You know, I'm still not exactly sure what happened...' I remarked.

'You were attacked by a venomous creature,' Anton cut in, 'an ancient monster that played with your perceptions, duping you into becoming an easy meal to slake its appetites.'

'You mean—Amalia?' I said.

'If that's the name it gave you,' Anton nodded. 'In fact, knowing its name could be of some advantage to us...'

'I think not,' Father Miklos broke in. He tore off a corner of his blotter and scratched momentarily on it with his pen. Capping it, he passed the fragment of paper across to Anton. The latter looked at it and raised his eyebrows.

'Ah. I see,' he said.

'Well, I certainly don't,' I growled, 'what's going on?' I snatched the scrap of paper from Anton's fingers and looked at it. There were three words and they read:

Amalia.

A Lamia.

'Means nothin' to me,' I muttered, dropping the scrap on the desktop in front of me.

'Mr Dolan,' Father Miklos sat forward and gestured expansively, like he was going into a sermon, 'a Lamia iss an ancient creature from very far back in Middle eastern culture, one that iss very dangerous and cruel. In Greece, we have legends of many similar creatures—the *vrykolatios*; the *mormo*; the *eretica*; the *callicantzaros*—but all of them stem from even older stories of an older creature, from the days of the Phoenicians which, in turn, come from even older mythologies than that. In short, Mr Dolan, the Lamia iss a vampire, which feeds off the life-force of other beings.'

'You're telling me that Amalia is some kind of bat?' I asked.

'No, no, no,' Miklos waved an admonishing finger, 'not a bat—it iss more like a snake.'

A sudden sense of revelation spread over me, causing me to fall back into my chair in a cold sweat. A slow-growing pressure of panic had been building inside me while Miklos was speaking, feeding my temper and making me antsy, but his last comment defused the sensation utterly like a popped balloon. I was suddenly aware why my skin had been crawling for no good reason at the *Fifty-Fifty Club* and I now knew why the good Father's sibilant esses were setting me on edge.

'Are you alright, Patrick? You've gone pale all of a sudden...' Anton placed a hand on my arm.

'I'll be fine,' I nodded, 'it's just a bit to take in all at once.'

'The poison of the creature iss difficult to overcome,' Miklos went on, 'it might be many more weeks before you're finally free of it.'

'Why didn't she just kill me straight out?' I asked.

Anton sat forward, shrugging. 'It's hard to fathom without being privy to her thought processes,' he said. 'I would hazard that each kill has the possibility of exposing the monster, so limiting the number of deaths around her lair lowers the possibility of her being discovered. Killing you immediately would be of short-term benefit; keeping you alive and draining you slowly offered a greater long-term advantage.'

'You're saying she likes to play with her food?' I snorted.

'It's a theory.'

'You and your theories!' I sat up again. 'What I want to know is what was with all that stuff at the *Fifty-Fifty Club*? And why was Archie Poole there? The last thing I recall was going to that burnt-out building and poking around for clues...'

Father Miklos said something in his own *patois* and shook his head chuckling.

'You were never at the *Fifty-Fifty Club*,' said Anton. 'We went to the ruined house and you went down into the cellar while I spoke with the night-watchman—whose name is John Cooper, by the way, not Archie. We went in search of you but couldn't find a trace. When we tried to go down the stairs into the earth after you, there was a terrible hissing and a baleful miasma rose up, threatening to poison us if we followed.'

'But...' I started.

Father Miklos leaned forward placing two fingers to the side of his brow.

'You saw many things, yes?' he said. 'Familiar people; a beautiful woman—all very real. The creature makes you see these things using its own mind: it feeds off your thoughts and memories and creates mirages to keep you subdued. None of it happened; but its poison made it seem as though it did, and it stopped you fighting against its will.'

I considered this. 'So, I went down into the cellar of that place and that was it? She pounced and you dragged me out again?' I gestured at Anton.

'Believe me,' he replied, 'it wasn't that easy. I tried several times to get down those steps to no avail. It wasn't until some-how you managed to be struggling up the stairs that we made a last-ditch effort and hauled you out.'

'That's because Archie told me to go there,' I said, 'I wouldn't have been near the stairs at all except that Archie told me where to go.'

The two of them looked at me blankly.

'Patrick,' said Anton, 'as I said, the only other person there that night was John Cooper the nightwatchman...'

I sat up, shaking my head. 'No, there was someone else,' I said. 'My friend Archibald Poole was at the club; he was work-ing there. When things started to go skew-whiff, he dragged me out into the kitchen and across to the stairwell. He made sure I got out, but he couldn't come with me because I'd put up that stupid ghost mirror...' I stopped, the wheels in my head turning slowly. The two of them exchanged a glance and looked back at me.

'Is it possible that Archie's *ghost* was there, looking after me?' I wondered.

Anton shrugged and looked across at Miklos. The latter mused momentarily, squinting and pursing his lips, then stood up and leaned towards me across the desk, bracing himself with his arms.

'I believe,' he said, feeling his way ahead carefully in his thoughts, 'that the creature was aware that you would be difficult to entrap. You are a worldly and cynical man, Mr Dolan, forgive my frankness, and not easily fooled by the things of this earthly life. The creature had to dig deep into your mind to bring forth images and situations which you would believe in and trust. To that end, it found in your memories a person—a guide—you would feel comfortable dealing with; a figure from your past you would not begin to suspect as being false. I think that the person it chose was one who was a great friend to you in your past life, but it did not count on the fact that your faith in that friend—and your memories of him—would be so strong that it could not but be an ally against the creature's machinations.' He nodded his head once, satisfied in his own theory, and sank back into his chair.

'I think there was no ghost to help you, Mr Dolan; there was only the strength of your own mind.'

I let that sink in.

'Then Archie *is* dead,' I murmured; 'I had it right all the time...'

'You see,' Anton leaned in, 'she chose the wrong person from your past memories to try and trick you. You knew that this Archie was dead, so your mind created a rationale to explain his presence, quite apart from the one that her scenario had imposed in order to make you think he was still alive. He was dead—but if he were a *ghost*, he could still walk the earth and circumvent that possibility. And your subconscious even provided ways to confirm this idea, with notions of haunting and of exorcisms—even the Chinese ghost mirror.'

'I set a booby-trap for him. I almost played right into her scaly hands…!'

'But you didn't, Mr Dolan. That's all that matters in the end. The rest iss—*poof!*— dreams and smoke.'

A telephone on a side cabinet jangled tinnily and Father Miklos turned to it quickly with an expression of annoyance. He picked up the receiver and spoke a few words into it, suddenly pleased by the message that was being conveyed. Then he listened, nodding, for a handful of moments, before speaking some more Greek and hanging the instrument up. He turned to face us, smiling, his fingers interlaced, arms resting on the desktop.

'Good news, gentlemen,' he beamed, 'members of my fraternity have just come from the creature's lair. It has been destroyed and the area consecrated—it will no longer be able to nest there.'

'What? They've killed her?' I gasped, sitting forward sharply.

'No,' replied the priest, 'unfortunately such beings are quite difficult to destroy. It has gone from there, however, and will not be able to return. They have found three bodies buried there as well, and the matter has been passed along to the local police. The creature will have to find a new place to dwell and establish a new routine, both of which will take some time, and which will test its fortitude. As you can see, it has suffered quite a setback.'

'Back to square one,' I said through gritted teeth.

Father Miklos twinkled his eyes at me. 'As you say.'

* * *

It was late and I was looking forward to my dinner. I had moved back into Anton's villa in Pott's Point. My landlady had figured that, after so many weeks' absence, I'd done a bunk, so she'd boxed up, sold off, or turfed out all my things and organised a new tenant. I'd had a few things to say to her when I found out and she'd had several to say in response; but the upshot was that I was living in Anton's spare room until I could sort out something else.

The evening was mild and the main reading room in the house was opened up to take advantage of the cool breeze and the perfumed air. North, towards the Harbour, the sky had turned brilliant orange and was now fading into a variegated pattern of moody red and purple. I put down my book and stared out past the shivering frangipani trees. Anton had given me a collection of Keats' poetry to read but I was having a hard time concentrating.

> "*She was a gordian shape of dazzling hue,*
>   *Vermilion-spotted, golden, green, and blue;*
> *Striped like a zebra, freckled like a pard,*
> *Eyed like a peacock, and all crimson barr'd;*
> *And full of silver moons, that, as she breathed,*
> *Dissolv'd, or brighter shone, or interwreathed*
> *Their lustres with the gloomier tapestries -*
> *So rainbow-sided, touch'd with miseries,*
> *She seem'd, at once, some penanced lady elf,*
> *Some demon's mistress, or the demon's self.*"

'What the Hell is a "gordian shape",' I muttered.

'I believe it refers to a complicated knot of ancient times, Mr Dolan,' Tegbir breezed into the room carrying a tray of tea things, 'apparently, Alexander the Great was quite vexed by his inability to untie it.'

'Best way to deal with a tangled mess is to just cut through it,' I opined, flipping pages.

'Yes, Mr Dolan,' Tegbir smiled through his luxurious black beard, 'I believe you have the trick of it.'

I stood up and walked over to the windows, looking out into the warm night as Tegbir made preparations to wheel in the samovar. Beneath the darkening sky, the city was all in blackness, save for the silver sheen of the water in the Harbour. Gentle winds stirred the flat, waxy frangipani leaves and rustled the rose gardens that surrounded the house. I took a deep breath of the sweet-smelling atmosphere...

I tensed. I'm not sure how I knew, but there was something out in the dark, hovering and unseen. My hackles rose—perhaps there was some kind of scent?—and I moved closer to the side of the French window, trying to get some kind of stability from its edge. I felt exposed, standing there in my braces and shirt sleeves, with nothing to defend myself...

'You left me.'

Her voice was petulant and throbbing. My mind was cast straight back to that terrible evening: her perfume wreathed about me as it had that night in the club, and I felt my pulse start to race. Vague in the darkness, scarcely illuminated by the light from within the house, I caught sight of her standing by the box hedge, her dress glittering as she softly moved, her eyes gleaming brilliant green and gold at me.

'I wanted you to stay.'

I breathed out raggedly. I hadn't even noticed that I was holding my breath in. My heart was hammering fit to burst. All my senses were responding to her "come hither" routine, but some deeper part of me—more primitive and better suited to keeping body and soul together—was telling me to cut and run.

'You wanted to eat me, you mean,' I gasped.

In the dark, she made a casual motion dismissing my remark.

'That too,' she said, *'but it would have been magnificent until it was over.'*

I scoffed.

'And you thought that's what I wanted?'

'It's what you all want… in the end.'

'It wouldn't have been real though, would it?'

Again, the dismissal.

'It would have been real in all the ways that matter. And you wouldn't have known the difference.'

'…Because you'd be messing with my head. Turns out, my mind was tougher than you'd expected, wasn't it?'

There was a lashing sensation out there in the black, like a large angry cat just twitched its tail in annoyance.

'I won't underestimate you this time…' There was an unpleasant, and bloody, edge to her voice now.

My left thigh began to twitch violently, causing my kneecap to jump as my body decided that it'd had enough. I sidled around the edge of the window trying to get out of view.

'Come out here, Patrick,' her voice had turned playful, alluring. *'There must be some way that we can come to terms…'*

'No way,' I answered, my teeth clicking together, 'you come into the light—I'm not going out there.'

I watched the glow from her eyes as she seemed to be scanning the wall of the house. *'I would, but there's... something...'*

I knew right then that Anton had done something to shield us within the building. If he'd been there right at that moment, I would've kissed him.

'Bugger off then, Lamia,' I said, with more courage than I felt, 'there's nothing for you here.'

Waves of anger seemed to wash over me as she hissed her displeasure.

'I will *leave,'* she spat, *'but, one day, I will come back, when you are without your friends and their silly tricks and then you and I will resolve matters altogether differently!'*

There was a gigantic rustling in the greenery, and she was gone. Outside the world was black and unfathomable.

I staggered backwards away from the French window, stumbling into the long table behind me. My heart was still pounding, and I was lathered in sweat. I ran a trembling hand over my face, and it came away bloody.

Behind me, I heard the rasp of steel and I looked around to see Tegbir re-sheathing his *kirpan*. He bustled over to me, keeping a wary eye on the windows, and eased me down into a chair.

'Are you alright, Mr Dolan?' he asked, matter-of-factly taking my pulse and checking my eyes.

'Yeah,' I nodded, catching my breath.

'Was it—?' he asked.

'Yes, it was,' I replied, shuddering.

He got up quickly and began closing all the windows one-by-one, swishing the curtains across them just to be sure. I took some more deep breaths astonished by how so much progress over the last many weeks had been undone by just a few moments.

'I was trying to move forward,' I muttered to myself, 'but I stepped on a snake...'

'I believe that there is no further cause for alarm, Mr Dolan,' Tegbir chirped, 'as the Guru says, *"Maya is not conquered, and the mind is not subdued"*'.

'...back to square one.' I closed my eyes.

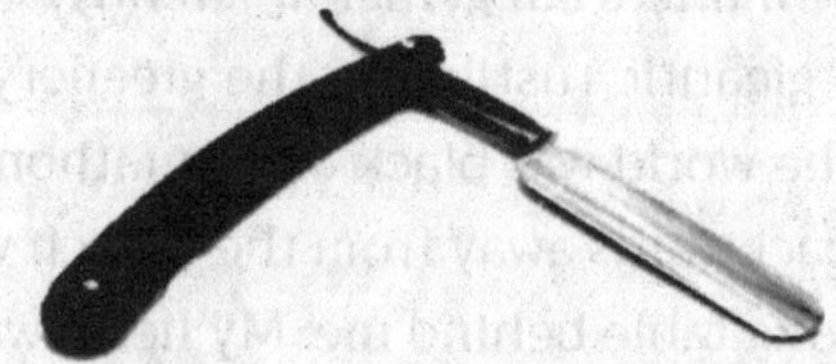

AFTERWORD

THE DEPRESSION
Sir Otto Niemeyer of the Bank of England advises lowering
Australia's "unjustified" high standard of living.
-Labor Daily, 1930

Sydney between the Wars was a desperate kind of a place. Having been "allowed" to assist Britain in turning back the tide of European aggression and going through a baptism of fire in order to do so, Australia was condemned to be jack-booted into national dysfunction by Commonwealth-appointed economic thugs determined to slice their own retirement fund out of this country's perceived "unjustified" high standard of living. In the aftermath of the Great War, two countries alone suffered the most devastating economic downturns ever experienced by a Western economy up to that point—Germany and Australia—and these were depressions deliberately inflicted upon them by other nations to serve their own vested interests.

The crippling poverty that struck this country manifested itself, in part, in the form of a criminal underworld in the heart of Sydney. This was a hotbed of gangsters and the drugs, illegal alcohol, prostitution and gambling that they brought with them. The activity focussed on that part of the city known as King's Cross and permeated out from there to Darlinghurst, Woolloomooloo, Paddington, The Rocks—even as far as Redfern. A gangster could be arrested for carrying a gun or a knife, but he couldn't be picked up for carrying a straight razor—a necessary item for any man trying to make a good impression in a hardscrabble world short of jobs—and the razor became the weapon of choice for gang members. The "razor gangs" proliferated in the murky underground of the sly-grog dens, two-up schools and whorehouses, a locale that the Press came to refer to as "Razorhurst".

My own interest in this lawless territory came from learning that a relative of mine had been shot dead there, mugged for two bottles of beer by a thug with a cheap gun and a heavy thirst. It seemed outrageous to me that such an act could have been perpetrated in the middle of a city patrolled by a fairly ruthless police force and that no verdict of justice was handed down afterwards. My great uncle had been shot and his killer had walked home, probably to share his trousered beer with his girlfriend, without a worry in the world. Crime unsolved.

Any of the books out there which describe the dark excesses of Razorhurst at this time (the 1920s through to the end of the 30s) has enough material to make even the most hardened writer of fiction's jaw drop to the pavement. I wondered—as is my wont—if all *this* was going on back then, what *else* could have been happening? Ideas of the evil that people do to each other led me to thinking what possibilities there might be for supernatural evil? The result is this series of tales.

There are those who might question why there are no stories here which showcase an Australian Indigenous perspective on the supernatural. I did think about it, but my understanding of the Aboriginal experience was too limited—in comparison to my extensive bibliographic understanding of the Western European magical tradition—and that it would be ill-served in my hands. Perhaps others, more suited to the task, could bring something to the table.

For now, I've paddled enough in this sordid wading pool and I think I've dragged from it all I need for the moment: Patrick and Anton may well reappear at some later date but, for now, I think I've put them through enough trauma. My intention here was to highlight a distant aspect of this country's history and demonstrate that it is a rich locale for storytelling—I hope that intention has played out as it should and I hope that you, the reader, have been entertained. That is—as always—my main objective.

ABOUT THE AUTHOR

Craig Stanton is a bookseller and writer who lives and works in the Blue Mountains west of Sydney. He has published two other collections of short stories – *Love Songs and Other Weirdness* and *Mountain Deviltry: Chilling Tales of the Blue Mountains* – and has been published in magazines and anthologies including the University of Newcastle's *SWAMP Anthology* and *"Occult Detective Magazine"*. He was a contributing writer, editor, and translator on the German horror comic *"Yuggoth Rising"*. When not penning short fiction, he maintains several blogs, including *The Miskatonic Debating Club & Literary Society* and *Moon of My Delight* which discusses his collection of copies of *The Rubaiyat of Omar Khayyam*. He has an online bookstore at ABEBooks, collaborates with many other booksellers across the Blue Mountains Bookshop Trail, and helps organise and promote the annual Blue Mountains Treasures Book Fair. He runs mostly on coffee.

EXPLORE NEW HORIZONS WITH US
AS WE SAIL ONTO SHORES OF LAT-
EST PRODUCTS, EVENTS, GREAT TI-
TLES, AND BEYOND.

VISIT US:
WWW.OCEANIACOM.COM

OCEANIACOM PRESS